SECRET
AGENTS
FOUR

Also by
DONALD J. SOBOL

SECRET AGENTS FOUR

Donald J. Sobol

Illustrated by Leonard Shortall

AN
APPLE
PAPERBACK

SCHOLASTIC INC.
New York Toronto London Auckland Sydney

For Ray Gross

ISBN 0-590-40565-9

12 11 10 9 8 7 6 5 4 3 2 1   12   8 9/8 0 1 2 3/9

Printed in the U.S.A.   11

CONTENTS

1

A Stranger Appears

WE ALL KNEW it was going to be an exciting summer because Orv Davy got off to such a fast start.

Orv is Dade City's top boy inventor. His first explosion occurred the very afternoon school let out. The boiler of his snow remover invention blew up.

My name is Ken Mullins. Inventing with Orv is the best way I know to stay in shape for track. You can never be sure when you're going to have to jump, or how far.

When the smoke from the explosion cleared, I saw a strange man standing by Orv's back door.

I hadn't heard him approach. With pieces of concrete hitting garbage cans and trees, and things flying seven ways at once, it's not easy to hear footfalls. Besides, I had a feeling the man could sneak up on a panther. He tickled my curiosity. Usually a person wandering into the Davy back yard for the first time doesn't stay. He takes one look and lights out for home holding his head.

True, the man showed amazement. His eyeballs were going up and down. But that was because he was looking at Bo Johnson.

You don't look at Bo all at once. Bo is seven feet tall. You look at him two or three feet at a time. As a sopho-more at Dade City High School, Bo was all teeth and ears. This past year he nearly quit growing and was named to the all-Florida basketball and baseball teams. Although he has filled out to two hundred and forty pounds, he can still go out on Halloween dressed as a wire coat hanger.

I wiggled from under a 1917 Ford touring car, where I'd dived when Orv's boiler sounded ready to blow sky high. I saw Horseshoes Kates dusting himself off.

Horseshoes isn't named Horseshoes because he's lucky, though you might say anyone is lucky who helps Orv with his inventions and stays alive. Horse-shoes' real name is Jerry. But we haven't called him Jerry since he won the horseshoe pitching contest at the State Fair in eighth grade.

Orv, Bo, Horseshoes, and I are known around the neighborhood as the Volcanos. Some grownup stuck us with the nickname last year after Orv's rainmaking machine blew up five times in the same week.

I felt myself for lumps and broken bones. Nothing seemed in the wrong place. So I joined Bo and Horseshoes in searching for Orv.

Finding Orv after an explosion is always tough. He's small for sixteen, as if his head were all that mattered and the rest of him was there just to carry his brains around. We saw him curled under a 1909 Hupmobile parts car.

He was mumbling to himself.

"I should have waited another week," he said to us. "Another week, and I'd have had it perfect!"

As Orv crawled out, a man's voice called to us.

I'd nearly forgotten about the stranger.

"Say, you boys do all this yourselves?" he asked.

"No," said Orv. "My dad does. He restores antique cars. That's his business."

Nodding his head in wonder, the man stared at the old cars in the Davy back yard.

Parked on the grass were a 1927 Packard sedan, a 1925 Kissel enclosed speedster, and the Hupmobile and Ford which Orv and I had used for bomb shelters.

The cars looked as if they had fallen a couple of miles through a can opener. Yet in a year they'd pass for brand-new. Mr. Davy is a magician. He rebuilds old cars so beautifully they could have their own TV shows.

Five more cars in different stages of rebuilding were in the row of sheds. And of course Big Dog was in the paint barn.

Big Dog was a 1930 Lincoln town car. Mr. Davy was getting it ready for Mr. Vorhoose to enter in car shows.

When Mr. Vorhoose hauled it into Mr. Davy's shop on a trailer last July, it looked like an escapee from the law of gravity. It was rusty and saggy, and I couldn't figure out what held it up. Everyone called it a dog, except Orv. Because it weighed three tons, Orv called it Big Dog.

Now Big Dog was nearly finished. All Mr. Davy had to do was rub the blue and black lacquer paint, put on the French gray striping, and hook up the battery.

The stranger took off his Panama hat and wiped the perspiration from his bald head.

"Hot day, isn't it?" he said nervously.

"It was a lot hotter around here three minutes ago," said Horseshoes.

It wasn't really a hot day. It was only eighty degrees. For Florida in June that's barely warm enough to swim.

"Your father has quite a tidy business," said the man. "Florida is perfect — perfect weather for it — for anything. You can keep cars outside all year around. You don't have to worry about shoveling snow off them or having the engines freeze up and crack."

He put his hat atop his head and continued to rattle on, as if somebody had pressed a button.

"I've lived on Miami Beach for seventeen years," he said. "I wish I'd come down here ten years earlier, yes, indeedy! Sell plating equipment — that's my line, boys. Cover all of southern Florida myself. Tampa to Melbourne to Key West. Maybe I can interest your father. Finest —"

"Dad's up in Jacksonville," said Orv. "Mr. Vorhoose asked him to look over a Buick. It's a one-of-a-kind. He'll be back late tonight."

"Too bad," said the man. "Well, another time. I just dropped by to ask a favor. May I use your telephone? I stopped to ask at a couple of houses down the road, but nobody was at home."

"A lot of families in this neighborhood head north for the summer on the day school lets out," I said.

"Well, I'd be mighty obliged if I could make a telephone call," said the man.

"Go right ahead," said Orv, pointing to the wall telephone by his dad's lathe.

Orv, Horseshoes, and Bo headed for the pillbox. Orv's dad had built it for him out of cement blocks when Orv began inventing seven years ago. We call it the pillbox because it would take an atomic bomb to budge it.

I was about to follow when I noticed that a handle

from the boiler had landed on the driveway. I started for it and passed the telephone. The stranger had finished dialing.

I heard him say, "Hello . . ." Then he pressed his lips together and just listened.

I picked up the handle from the driveway. That's when I noticed his car parked on the street. The license plates were from New Jersey. But I was too interested in getting back to the pillbox and finding out what had gone wrong with Orv's snow-remover invention to think much about license plates then.

When I passed the stranger again, he was still listening, and wiping the top of his head.

The inside of the pillbox was worse than a junk yard with hiccups. Most of the machinery lay scattered over the floor. The rest hung here and there from the ceiling and walls. Orv's brave dream of helping the American people up north remove snow from their sidewalks had gone *frrrrwhoompppp!* When I thought how lucky we were to have made it out the door before everything blew, I began to shake like a dust mop.

Orv poked around moodily.

"Cheer up, Orv," I said. "With a little more testing, it would have worked fine."

I meant every word. Orv's snow remover was the greatest idea since the shovel — on paper.

It consisted of hot water pipes under the sidewalk

to melt the snow. A boiler heated the water in the pipes and also powered a system of jacks and gears. When the snow melted, the sidewalk tipped and the melting snow slid off. It was pure genius. Only the boiler hadn't done its part.

Bo began to stack pieces of the model sidewalk by the door. Horseshoes had picked up a handful of twisted gears and was pitching them into a corner. He put a little spin on his throws for practice, but his heart wasn't in it.

After ten minutes we had most of the mess heaped in a pile, along with our dreams of becoming millionaires.

Bo paused by the door. "Hey," he said. "That man is sure interested in Big Dog."

The stranger hadn't departed. He was in the paint barn crouched by Big Dog.

"I think he's caught sight of us," whispered Bo.

The stranger suddenly stepped back, as if to admire the car's sweeping lines.

"He's not admiring. He's snooping," said Horseshoes.

Orv's dad never chased anybody away from his cars, even though a fingernail scratch could ruin a paint job which had taken him days to bring to a mirrorlike gleam. Mr. Davy had a lot of faith. He said people respected beauty and wouldn't touch his cars. So far he'd been right.

But the stranger had gone into the paint barn without

a by-your-leave. Maybe I'm the suspicious type (I forgot to mention that I'm going to be a secret agent), but I felt sure he was up to something.

"I'd better see if I can help him," said Orv.

Like his father, Orv always thought the best of everyone.

"We'll come with you," I said grimly.

We followed Orv out of the pillbox. I hadn't an inkling of what lay ahead. I sort of counted on Bo in case of trouble.

Bo never raised his fists in anger. If a fight came to him, he had a trick of winning all his own. He snarled. He pulled himself up to his full seven feet and snarled. It was enough to make a troop of cavalry head for deep water.

We marched across the grass toward the paint barn, a distance of a hundred yards as you measure land.

Measured by what eventually happened to the four of us, it was a walk right onto a battlefield.

2

Hot in Pursuit

THE STRANGER WATCHED as four sixteen-year-old boys came toward him. His eyes narrowed briefly. Then he broke out the soapiest grin this side of Election Day.

"What a car!" he said, dripping friendliness all over Big Dog. "I'd love to hear the motor. Can you start her up?"

"I'm sorry," said Orv. "She's not ready. Besides, Mr. Vorhoose, who owns the car, is kind of particular. He won't let Dad start her. He won't even let Dad hook up the battery."

"Why not?" asked the stranger.

"Mr. Vorhoose insists on being the first to start the engine of any car my dad restores for him," said Orv.

The stranger's gaze drifted to the new battery resting on the floor beside Big Dog. We stood around hoping he'd leave without being asked. The situation had reached the feet-shuffling stage before he turned to go.

"Thanks for the use of the telephone," he said to Orv. "So long, fellows."

After he'd gone, Bo said, "There was something funny about that man. I wonder what he really wanted."

"He wanted to look over Big Dog. He's a car spy," I said, putting a couple of clues together.

"Man," said Bo, "that last explosion loosened your tacks."

"You're forgetting that some people who own fine old cars put winning a trophy before the fun of the hobby," I said. "They won't enter a show if they can't win. So if a car is going to be shown for the first time, like Big Dog, they send a spy around to find out how good it is."

Orv shook his head in disbelief. "Dad's never had a car spy here before."

"Five days from today there will be two car shows in Florida," I reminded Orv. "The Orlando Antique Car Meet and the Reservoir City Meet. Some owners will sign up for both shows. But they will enter their cars only in the one they think they can win."

"There's no telling what that man did to Big Dog," said Horseshoes nervously. "He was alone in the paint barn for several minutes."

"And try this," I said. "He claims to have lived in Miami Beach for seventeen years."

"You can prove he isn't telling the truth?" demanded Orv. "How?"

"By his head," I retorted. "It was wetter than the transatlantic cable. What Floridian perspires in only eighty degree heat? None! Only Northerners who come to visit do. And his license plates are from New Jersey!"

Orv suddenly looked worried.

We heard the stranger's car pulling away from the front of the house.

"We're wasting time," said Bo. "Let's follow him!"

We raced for the Rod. I slipped behind the wheel as Orv bounded into the front seat beside me. Bo curled up in back, and Horseshoes wiggled till he found some room where Bo's knees weren't.

I turned the Rod west on Rolling Road, the direction the stranger's blue car had been facing. It was all I could do to keep under the speed limit.

At the traffic light where Rolling Road crossed Cutler Avenue, four cars waited.

"There he is!" I bellowed. "The blue car — second in line."

The green signal lighted. The blue car turned north on Cutler Avenue toward Miami, sixteen miles away. I turned with it.

"Keep him in sight," said Horseshoes. "Don't let him see us."

Orv and I chuckled. The Rod is a 1930 Ford town sedan, about ten inches higher than a modern car. The stranger couldn't help seeing us in his rearview mirror.

I trailed him for ten minutes, waiting for a hint that he had spotted us. Suddenly he turned right into a little side street. I wasn't sure till he drove two blocks, turned left, and left again. We were back on Cutler, traveling faster.

"He's seen us!" I called.

We were approaching downtown Miami. The traffic grew thicker. The blue car again tried to shake us. But I hung to it through a jigsaw course of five blocks.

"This is going to be interesting," I said.

"I'll tell you something else that's interesting," said Horseshoes. "*We're* being followed."

"Police?" I gasped.

"No, unless the police have taken to driving around in big black cars," he said.

All at once I had misgivings about the man in the blue car. Who *was* he?

Before I had a chance to worry myself sick, the blue car tried again to give us the slip.

It circled three blocks, dodging in and out of traffic and disobeying two stop signs. I lost ground but kept it in sight.

"Is that black car still behind us?" I yelled.

"Like a tailgate," answered Bo.

Ahead the blue car had raced across a bridge over the Miami River. Reaching the other side, it screeched into a sliding turn, stones spurting from under the rear tires.

I had a glimpse of the fright on the stranger's face as he glanced in our direction. Then the blue car roared down a narrow gravel road that hugged the riverbank.

The stranger had blundered. The gravel road went for a hundred yards and no more. It stopped at a warehouse entrance. A dead end!

I shifted down, and the Rod took the turn at the base of the bridge smartly. We had the stranger blocked.

"Don't make any sudden moves," said Orv in a weak little voice.

"Huh?" I said. "What?"

"One of the men in the black car is pointing a gun, and it's too big for a water pistol," explained Orv.

There was a startling *bang!*

The stranger jumped out of the blue car as if he had kangaroo blood in his legs.

"Let's tell them everything they want to know about Big Dog," urged Horseshoes. "Mr. Davy would want us to be truthful."

"If we get out with our hands up, they'd see we were only a bunch of harmless, mixed-up teenagers," said

Bo. "We could say we were chasing an ice cream truck and got lost in traffic."

I rammed down the brake pedal, and we went for the door handles. It's not easy to open a door with your two hands raised, believe me.

Horseshoes tumbled out first. He held his hands above his head and tried like crazy to look innocent. If I hadn't felt the same color streaking down my spine, I'd have called him a name.

I faced around as the black car stopped inches behind the Rod. Four pistols emerged, followed by four very big men.

The biggest of the four charged straight for me.

3

Mongoose versus Cobra

THE BIG MAN was upon me. All I could see was his Adam's apple bouncing atop his shirt collar.

I heard a pistol shot and something struck me in the right shoulder and spun me around like a pastry plate. I fell flat on my face.

"I've been killed!" I thought wildly. "I've been killed! I'll never live to be seventeen!"

Clutching my shoulder, I rolled on my back — I didn't want to die with my nose in the gravel. Orv, Bo, and Horseshoes bellywhopped under the Rod. Luckily, they'd had plenty of practice fleeing Orv's experiments. They dived like experts.

Shots exploded around us. Gradually they grew

more distant. I recovered myself somewhat. I pulled my hand from my shoulder to look at my blood-soaked fingers, but I saw only a few scratches from the gravel. It was a bit disappointing.

I wasn't dying. I wasn't even shot.

I scrambled up, overjoyed at the big man's terrible aim. He came charging at me again, his gun smoking and his head down.

"Oh, no," I thought, and dropped on my back before he had a second crack at me.

"Sorry to have bumped you, son," he panted, racing by.

He pulled a speaker from his car. He talked into it like a radio announcer being paid by the word. He spoke so fast I had to wiggle my ears to understand him.

He was making a report. He said "he" got away from "us." He described Orv, Bo, Horseshoes, me, the Rod, and the place where we were.

As he put back the speaker, his three companions returned, fitting their pistols into shoulder holsters. The four of them climbed silently into the big black car and sped off.

On the drive to Orv's house, everyone offered an explanation.

I had the feeling that the four men were from Mongoose, the government's top secret counterspy agency. Why they were chasing the man in the blue car was

beyond me, however. As I had only a hunch about Mongoose, I didn't tell the others.

It was five o'clock when I drove the Rod home. My ears were still ringing with explanations of the gun battle. I got out a light snack. It was near dinner, and I didn't want to ruin my appetite.

I took a banana and a glass of milk and some brownies to the kitchen table and sat down in front of Mom's knickknack shelf. The shelf holds four hand-painted dishes and Orv's first invention — a butter knife with two blades and the handle in the center. Orv gave it to Mom seven years ago when the twins were born. Mom said it was too beautiful to use. She put it up on the shelf to keep forever.

My thoughts drifted to Orv. Whenever I have a feeling I'm in for trouble in a grown-up world, it's comforting to know a boy like Orv. He can really help grownups solve their problems. And if my hunch was correct, Orv, Bo, Horseshoes, and I were in for a truckload of trouble.

I ought to say a little more about Orv. First off, he always does the nice thing.

For example, last winter Reverend Willard was leaving on a trip to Boston. Orv gave him an umbrella with a whistle attached so the reverend could call a cab in the rain easily. Orv also gave him a hat with a rim that wasn't attached so the reverend could tip it without catching cold.

For my dad, Orv made a special throw rug. Occasionally Dad walks in his sleep. The rug has an electric alarm sewn inside which rings and wakes Dad whenever he sleepwalks. Orv brought it over to the house right after the trouble at the Navy base at Ocheebo Creek.

Until the Ocheebo Creek trouble, I thought Dad worked for the Post Office Department. Then Orv's rocket experiment went haywire, and the missile landed seven miles away, square in the Navy's top secret Ocheebo Creek base. At first the local police decided the missile must be some kind of detector sent over by an enemy power. Dad brought it home and questioned me for an hour about Orv. That's when I learned Dad wasn't a postal inspector. He was assistant chief of the Miami bureau of Mongoose, our government's special agency for fighting the worldwide organization of master criminals known as Cobra.

Very few people know about Cobra. Only small nations felt Cobra's fangs — in the beginning. As each new crime fattened its treasury, Cobra grew larger, stronger, and bolder. Today, Cobra has agents in every major country.

"You're worrying over nothing," I told myself. "The

stranger probably stole the blue car. The four men in the black car chasing him were Dade City detectives."

But it was like trying to convince myself I never got hungry before dinner.

I ate another banana and cleaned up the kitchen before Mom got home with the twins. They arrived as I flipped the peels into the garbage bag from twelve feet.

"Ken," said Mom, kissing me, "don't forget, you're baby-sitting tonight. Dad and I are going to the theater after dinner. We'll be at the playhouse in Coconut Grove. The number is on the pad."

I said how happy I was to watch Jean and Jane go to sleep on the first night of summer vacation. If I were any happier, I'd have sat down in the rocking chair and cried.

However, I never did baby-sit with my sisters that evening. Dad came home an hour late. He spoke gravely to Mom in the hall outside the bathroom. I heard the name John McGrath, who is Dad's boss at Mongoose. Then Mom shrugged and said she needed an evening alone. She said she had to catch up on her sewing, and she wouldn't have liked the play anyway.

During dinner the twins jabbered and fought while Mom, Dad, and I sat around and pretended nothing was in the air. Dad never once asked me what I'd done with myself all day. I figured he knew very well.

After I'd helped Mom clear the dinner dishes, Dad suggested I call Mary Evans and take her somewhere. I said I didn't want to waste the summer fooling around. I had a lot of reading to do. I wanted to improve my mind.

I went to my room and selected a book and waited for Mr. McGrath to arrive. The doorbell rang at ten o'clock and saved me from going cross-eyed staring at the same page.

Dad greeted his chief at Mongoose, and Mr. McGrath apologized.

"I'm sorry, Carl," he said to Dad. "But we had better talk this over right away. Good heavens! We fumbled it! And we were so close!"

"We can talk in the living room, John," said Dad.

My bedroom is next to the living room. I had kept my door open to a crack wider than my left ear, which is flatter than my right, because I sleep on that side. Although Dad and Mr. McGrath practically whispered, I heard them clearly.

Dad and Mr. McGrath discussed the chase and the stranger's escape. The more I heard, the worse I felt.

The stranger was Max Ripley, a low-level Cobra. Mongoose agents had been following him for days, hoping he would lead them to Cobra headquarters in the United States. When Max Ripley had spied the Rod trailing him, he had also, Dad said, seen the black car with Mongoose agents. Then all Dad's hard work had been spoiled by four teenagers playing detective.

"I spoke with Orville Davy this afternoon," said Dad. "What happened was a freak bit of chance. Max Ripley stopped at the Davy house to make a telephone call. He stayed a few minutes to admire an antique Lincoln called Big Dog. Orville and three friends — one of them my own son Ken — believed he was a car spy and pursued him."

"What about the telephone call Ripley made?" asked Mr. McGrath.

"It was a local call and so can't be traced," said Dad. "The person to whom Ripley spoke is in the greater Miami area some place. That tells us nothing we didn't already know."

Dad and Mr. McGrath talked anxiously for several minutes. Although I couldn't follow all the threads of their conversation, I learned one frightening fact. Cobra had demanded the United States pay ten million dollars by the fifteenth of June — five days hence. If the money wasn't paid, something more dreadful than an atomic bombing was going to befall Miami.

Suddenly Mr. McGrath said, "Orville Davy . . . Orville Davy! My goodness, not the *same* boy!"

"Yes," said Dad ruefully. "The same boy who fired the rocket into the Navy's Ocheebo Creek installation last year."

"He's a human catastrophe!" said Mr. McGrath in a rising voice. I imagined the color of his face was rising too.

"Orville is very promising," said Dad.

I heard a chair squeak and then footsteps. Mr. McGrath was pacing the floor.

"Get his father to send him away," ordered Mr. McGrath. "Iceland is ideal for promising boys this time of year."

"Fred Davy can't afford the expense," said Dad.

"Okay, what about camp? Maine has a lot of good camps — builds muscles, develops character," said Mr. McGrath. "Better yet, Canada."

"Fred Davy won't let Orv go," said Dad. "Orv helps him around the shop. Then he has his experiments and his airplane."

"He flies his own airplane?"

Dad hesitated before explaining about Orv's plane. It was a World War I De Havilland.

"I might have known!" roared Mr. McGrath.

He resumed tramping the carpet. All at once he shouted, "If you can't beat 'em, join 'em!"

"Enlist a sixteen-year-old boy as a Mongoose agent?" said Dad, astonished.

"Make him think so," replied Mr. McGrath. "Make him think so."

"I don't like it, John," said Dad solemnly.

"Now see here, Carl. That one boy is a menace to our entire organization. Today in twenty minutes he undid the work of a year."

"My own son was equally to blame," said Dad. "Besides, the boy might get hurt."

"That's the whole point," asserted McGrath. "Give him a duty that will keep him out of harm's path — and out of our hair!"

"I could assign him to inventing," said Dad after a long pause.

"Have him invent something that will require a couple of years," urged Mr. McGrath.

Another long pause and Dad said, "John, I've got it! I'll have him invent — a spy-catching machine!"

"*A spy-catching machine!* Carl, that's absolute inspiration."

"I'll talk with the boy in the morning," said Dad.

I thought, "If Orv sets his mind to inventing a spy-catching machine, he'll invent one. Cobra is a cooked goose!"

I couldn't wait for morning.

4

Secret Agents Four

THE NEXT MORNING Dad came into the Davys' yard and thanked Orv, Bo, Horseshoes, and me. He said we had shown great courage in pursuing a Cobra agent unarmed.

Orv, Bo, and Horseshoes swelled with amazement and pride. I nearly believed Dad. He made it sound as if we'd done our country a service instead of fouling up Mongoose.

Dad spoke about Mongoose and Cobra. He explained that Cobra was preparing a mysterious and deadly blow against the city of Miami unless the government paid ten million dollars by the fifteenth day of June. He asked for a machine to foil Cobra's evil plot — a machine to catch spies. Could Orv invent one in four days?

"It's a difficult assignment," said Orv doubtfully. But I'd never seen him look so excited. "Thank you for the opportunity," he said. "I shall do my best."

After Dad left, we pondered what Cobra was up to. Orv grew bored.

"Fellows," he said. "I have to do some thinking. It's on the subject of a new use of Davy-power. So please excuse me."

Davy-power is Orv's one secret — the only part of his inventing he won't share. When he experiments with it, we are glad to treat him as if he has mumps.

He disappeared into the pillbox. Bo, Horseshoes, and I discussed the difficulties of counterspying.

"We ought to learn judo or karate," I said. "What if Cobra agents attack us and Bo isn't around?"

"Run," suggested Horseshoes. "You're a sprinter."

"You'll sing another tune if a Cobra agent sticks a gun in your ribs," I said.

"Okay," said Horseshoes, stretching on the grass. He cupped his hands under his head. "Go learn the gentle art of self-defense. Call Mary Evans."

I had walked into that one with my chin stuck out like a kitchen drawer.

Mary is the prettiest girl in our class and an expert in self-defense. She and I had been going steady, more or less, for two months.

That night I asked her to give me a cram course in

karate or judo or jiujitsu. "Whichever it is," I said, "that makes the bad guys fly around like loose paint."

She agreed a trifle too happily.

In the morning she showed up at Orv's wearing a white long-sleeved blouse, white trousers, and a brown belt tied around her middle.

"Good and soft," she said, feeling the grass. "This morning I shall teach you to fall forward."

"I want to make the *other fellow* fall," I corrected.

"*Hai!*" growled Mary. My feet left the ground and she guided me through the air so that I landed on my side.

"I wasn't ready!" I protested. Still, I got the point in a hurry.

"A simple *okui-as-barai*," she said. "A side-foot sweep. Always take care to come down on your side and not your back."

I fell all morning.

Around eleven o'clock Mr. Davy slid from under the Hupmobile. He saw me beating the ground with my forearms and hastened into the house. He brought out Mrs. Davy. They stared at me to make sure they weren't dreaming.

At noon Mrs. Davy served us lunch. Her lips parted when she laid down my plate. She wanted to say something motherly but couldn't find the words.

After we'd eaten, everyone went back to his station.

Orv was working in the garage. Horseshoes and Bo settled behind their spy novels, the fakers. I faced Mary
impatiently.

"Teach me some throws — *now!*" I said.

"You won't learn," said Mary with a hopeless shake
of her blonde head. She tensed and hissed, "*Sa!*"

"*Sa!*" I thought, might mean "*Hai!*" and I knew what
that meant.

As Mary's hands darted for my collar, I ended my
judo lessons by side-stepping. I spun her around by the
shoulders and lifted her off the ground with an old-
fashioned full-nelson.

"Put me down!" she screamed, kicking her bare heels
into my shins.

I put her down, gently.

"Ken Mullins," she cried. "That was my best *tachi-
waza!*"

Her voice was scolding, and yet her eyes were wider
and bluer than I'd ever seen them. I had a feeling we'd
be going steady steady after today.

As we stood mooning at each other, Orv opened the
garage door.

"Come help me with my spy-catching machine," he
called.

Bo, Horseshoes, Mary, and I rolled the Rod out to the
open span of grass behind the pillbox. Orv set two jack
stands under the rear axle.

"Keep clear of the rear wheels. They're hooked up to Davy-power," he warned, climbing into the driver's seat. "Ordinarily, to start a car you must turn the ignition key to the right. I'm going to start the motor by turning the key to the left."

He let the motor run a few moments and killed it.

"Imagine one of Cobra's agents hotly pursued by Mongoose," he said. "Desperate to get away, he jumps into the Rod and turns the key — to the *right*."

A thunderous *whoooossshh!*

The rear wheels blew off like smoke rings and landed eight feet away. The Rod dipped onto the jack stands and there remained, forlornly seated.

Silently Bo helped Orv climb out. Horseshoes and I got the wheels back on without exchanging opinions.

"You don't think much of it," said Orv lamely.

"Orv," said Bo. "Suppose the Cobra agent doesn't jump into the Rod? Suppose he jumps into his own car?"

"It's corny," admitted Orv.

"The strain of spy-catching has got us all," said Bo. "I move we go fishing tomorrow. Let Mongoose carry on alone against Cobra one more day."

The motion passed, and we were about to part when Horseshoes raised a point.

"We ought to have a name," he said. "Every organization of secret agents has a name."

"We have a name — the Volcanos," I said, referring to the title given us in the neighborhood.

"That was our inventors' name," objected Horseshoes. "We're counterspies now. We haven't blown up anything as counterspies."

"Give us time," said Bo.

Horseshoes persisted. "Volcanos doesn't have any periods like the names of spy groups on television," he said. "If it were V.O.L.C.A.N.O.S. and stood for something, I'd vote for it."

I said, "It could stand for Victorious Operators Lawfully Campaigning Against — " That was as far as I could get.

Horseshoes was holding his nose.

"How's this," offered Bo. "Verbs Of Local Community Act Nervelessly On Sinners."

"*Verbs?*" cried Horseshoes.

"I couldn't think of a noun beginning with V," replied Bo.

Horseshoes held his nose and shook his head.

Mary tried one. "Valiant Officers Lately Called A Nuisance Oppose Scoundrels."

"It would make a good newspaper headline," said Horseshoes gallantly. "Anything from you, Orv?"

"Well," said Orv. "How about, Very Often Loathesome Criminals Are Nabbed Outdoors Society."

It was the best yet, but unquestionably terrible.

"Forget Volcanos," suggested Horseshoes. "Start with a meaning."

We sat around forgetting Volcanos. For half an hour we sat and forgot.

"Aw, let's give it up," said Bo. "Maybe tomorrow —"

"Wait!" said Horseshoes. "I think I've got it."

He jumped up, his face aglow.

"Volunteer Agents Crusading Unsteadily Under Mongoose," he crowed.

For a split second the rest of us were held silent by a thrill of admiration.

Then we shouted together, "V.A.C.U.U.M.!"

It was a brainstorm, a name to march beside the C.I.A. and the F.B.I.

But Horseshoes wasn't done. He moved we admit Mary as a "Beautiful Assistant Gangbuster," by which he triumphantly arrived at her full title, V.A.C.U.U.M. B.A.G.

Mary laughingly accepted her admittance into the only teenage counterspy society in America. So named and content, we parted till it was time to go fishing.

I had the sleep rubbed out of my eyes and the sandwiches Mom had made tucked under my arm when Horseshoes drove up hauling his family's boat. It's a seventeen-foot runabout fitted with twin forty-five horsepower outboards.

Bo and Orv were in the back of the car, half asleep. We stopped for Mary, who supplied the sodas, and slipped the boat into the water at the Dinner Key marina.

We had planned to go salt water fishing in the bay. But a thirty-mile-an-hour wind was chopping up three-foot waves. So we cruised along the coast and swung into the Miami River after bass.

We would have forgotten all about spying if it hadn't been for a loony barracuda. It must have been part salmon, for it was swimming upriver toward fresh water.

Bo saw it first and couldn't do a thing. He had only a bamboo pole and line for bottom fishing. I had the helm. Mary was holding the navigation chart. Horseshoes was snoozing.

That put it squarely up to Orv and his wonderful Davy-powered fishing rod.

Orv's rod casts and winds at the touch of a button. Squeeze another button and a fishnet pops out. Still another button works a tiny camera for photographing the big one that got away.

"Barracuda at one o'clock," hollered Bo. "Get 'em, Orv!"

Orv sighted along the rod and squeezed. The line whizzed out. The lead sinker flashed in the sun and disappeared with a *blurp!* right by the barracuda.

Orv reeled in by hand. The barracuda floated a little

below the surface. I steered alongside. Bo leaned over and hauled it aboard.

"It's a good five feet long!" he whooped.

It was the biggest barracuda ever knocked unconscious in the Miami River. All of us cheered except Orv.

"Luck," he said. He looked thoughtfully upon the barracuda. "Luck is part of fishing, but not of inventing. I hoped to get lucky with my wheel-remover. That was a mistake. I ought to have studied the only spy we've met. The stranger in the blue car."

"It's a little late," said Horseshoes. "He's long gone."

"We can bring him back," said Orv, "in memory. He walked up the driveway and asked to use the telephone. He said he had tried a couple of houses on the block, but nobody was at home."

Orv raised his hands and grinned. "Oh, you don't have to tell me why. Half the neighborhood takes to the hills of North Carolina the minute school is out and I begin experimenting full time."

"Get back to the stranger," said Horseshoes.

"Okay," replied Orv. "He used the telephone and while we were in the pillbox he slipped into the paint barn with Big Dog. However, he didn't do any damage because he wasn't the simple car spy we thought. He was a full-fledged Cobra agent. Besides, my dad checked Big Dog carefully. There's nothing missing or damaged."

"The stranger might have been just admiring Big Dog," I said. "But your father can't be sure everything works till Mr. Vorhoose lets him hook up a battery and runs the engine."

"Granted," said Orv. "However, the stranger had only a few minutes alone with Big Dog, and that's not enough time to do any damage that doesn't show. Anyway, why would he bother? The real lead is his telephone call."

Bo snapped his fingers. "I follow you," he exclaimed. "The telephone company will have a record of his call even if he reversed charges!"

"We can find out to whom he spoke!" sang Horseshoes.

"Unless it was a local call," said Mary. "Then nobody has a record of it."

Orv, Bo, and Horseshoes glared at her.

The truth was going to hurt, but I had to tell them sooner or later. "It was a local call," I said. "I overheard my dad say so to Mr. McGrath."

Orv was crushed. "No record, no lead," he said.

"No lead, no case," said Bo.

"No nothing," said Horseshoes.

"No nothing, no V.A.C.U.U.M.," they said together. And their faces fell.

"We're fortunate the stranger made a local call," I told them.

The bells of never-say-die were chiming loud and

clear in my head. The hour had struck for the serious student of espionage to take over.

"Don't you understand?" I said. "It means that the person he was calling lives right here in Dade City. Why, he might have been speaking with Cobra headquarters!"

"What's our next move?" asked Bo skeptically. "Do we go around ringing twenty thousand doorbells and handcuff the first man who hisses at us?"

"We ring the most likely doorbell," I replied. "Mystery Island."

Orv made a face like a squeezed prune. "Everything that happens in Dade City that can't be explained is blamed on Mystery Island."

"We've fished near there plenty," objected Horseshoes. "It's completely encircled by stone walls twenty feet high. The only gate is by the dock, and the sign there says, 'Keep out!'"

"Mystery Island is in Dade City," I said stubbornly. "What is a more likely place for Cobra headquarters?"

"You ring the doorbell," said Horseshoes. "Something about that place makes me believe in signs."

"Maybe I will ring the doorbell," I said, "after we take a peek inside the walls."

I was prepared for their looks of surprise and added, "From the air."

5

Orv Takes to the Air

M Y PLAN was to reconnoiter Mystery Island without stirring the suspicions of Cobra or whoever dwelt there.

For the mission, V.A.C.U.U.M. would call upon two of its ace weapons: Bo's camera and Orv's World War I De Havilland DH-4 biplane.

"The Miami Antique Airplane Association will have a fly-in the day after tomorrow, according to the *Miami Journal*," I said. "The flight will start at Homestead Air Force Base and put down in Fort Lauderdale. The old planes will have to pass over — or nearly over — Mystery Island."

The scheme I had in mind was for Orv and Bo to join the flight in Orv's De Havilland. Nearing Mystery Island, Orv would make the motor cough like an epidemic. Seemingly forced off course by a failing motor, the De Havilland would veer over Mystery Island after the fashion of a dying swan, looping, circling, coughing, till Bo had finished his aerial photography.

"Of course, the people on the island will spot you," I said. "But when you fly away, they'll be too relieved to be angry or suspicious."

The scheme was approved, and before we docked the runabout at Dinner Key, we had the mission broken down. Each member of V.A.C.U.U.M. had his duty till Orv and Bo took off on their great motor failure act.

Bo went home to his dark room and dusted off his long-range lenses. Orv said he still had one last thought on Davy-power and holed up in the pillbox. Horseshoes spent the next day at the Dade City airstrip checking the plywood De Havilland for termites.

Mary was armed with sandwiches, milk, and a telescope and assigned to Dadeland Beach. There her job was to keep one end of the spyglass clapped to her eye and the other end pointed at Mystery Island, a mile off shore. If any hanky-panky was afoot, V.A.C.U.U.M. wanted to know at once.

For my part, I spent most of the next morning in the Miami Journal building. I went up to the morgue, which is the library where clippings of past newspapers are filed.

The librarian was very firm about the rules. She wouldn't let me near the files. She told me to be seated at a desk in the corner and asked me what I wanted to see.

"The Miami Off-Street Parking Board," I said.

"There are *two drawers* of clippings on that," she said.

I had guessed as much. There were probably even more clippings under "University of Miami" or "Cuba," but Miami Off-Street Parking Board was alphabetically close to Miblen's Island, which was the real name of Mystery Island. I wasn't going to let the librarian or anyone outside of V.A.C.U.U.M. learn I was interested in Mystery Island.

"I can only let you see one folder of clippings at a time," she said. "So what in particular do you want?"

"I'd like to see it all," I said. "Please."

I thought she muttered something under her breath. But she brought me the first folder and returned to her desk. After three minutes, I said I was done and would she mind terribly bringing me the next folder?

For half an hour she upheld the rules, tramping doggedly among the file cabinets, my desk, and hers every three minutes. Then her feet and her patience gave out.

"Oh, go help yourself," she barked, or her feet did.

I sped between the rows of file cabinets and bent over. Thus hidden from the librarian, I replaced the Miami Off-Street Parking Board folder. Almost in the same motion, I opened a drawer to the right, found the folder marked Miblen's Island, and carried it to my spot in the corner. I felt as if I'd acquired full rights to Captain Kidd's buried treasure in return for a leaky bucket and two used cannonballs.

I opened the folder. Before me lay the history of Miblen's — or Mystery — Island.

The forty acres had been first settled in 1887 by a cow doctor named Emanuel Pasteur Miblen. With the help of some wandering Indians, he had constructed the twenty-foot walls in order to conduct secret animal experiments. Hoping to produce through crossbreeding a hunting dog that could fly, he stocked the island with gulls and setters. Alas, he produced only gutters. And as these soon became the laughing stock of the county he cast himself upon the tide and was never heard from again.

Such was the legendary beginning of the island. In 1892 it became an old age home for Civil War veterans. After 1920 the island changed owners every few years. The present owner was a German, Mr. Hans Schnitzer. He never stepped upon the mainland. Save for a weekly visit by a magnificent yacht, no movement or sign of life was observed outside the walls. Mr. Schnitzer was a mystery, and the name Mystery Island had become affixed to the place.

I jotted down everything in my notebook. At Orv's

house that evening V.A.C.U.U.M. heard my findings.

"It looks mighty suspicious," said Horseshoes. "That Schnitzer is probably crossbreeding a little wine with pretzels to get wiener schnitzels."

"Be serious," said Bo.

"We'll know everything in the morning," said Orv.

Rain was falling as I climbed into my pajamas, and a light drizzle still sprayed my window when my alarm clock rang in the morning. I telephoned Orv. He assured me the antique plane fly-in would take place, rain or shine. V.A.C.U.U.M. would photograph the inside of Mr. Schnitzer's island.

Orv, Bo, and Horseshoes went out to the airstrip. Mary and I drove to Dadeland Beach to watch Orv do his acrobatics over the island. We were alighting from the Rod when the clouds parted. The full face of the sun blazed down.

A few minutes past nine o'clock we heard a horrible roar. We saw the lead planes, a pair of World War II trainers, flying toward us. Behind them limped five early racers. Strung farther behind were a dozen boxy aircraft that might have been glued together by a small boy in bed with fever. In the rear, stuttering and staggering, were two motor-driven crates which the Wright brothers had refused to ride in. It was a fine, inspiring sight.

Orv's orange and green De Havilland appeared as

the lead planes in the formation passed overhead, on course to Fort Lauderdale.

Through binoculars, I saw poor Bo curled up in the cockpit holding his camera above his helmet for lack of space. Orv was throttling down. The motor coughed and I thought a battle leer widened his lips.

"He's pretending he's in a dogfight over France!" I cried to Mary. "For Pete sake, Orv, don't forget what you're doing!"

The De Havilland had banked and was swooping for Mystery Island. At the last split-second Orv pulled it up. The wheels passed six inches above the wall.

"Bo should have a good close-up from that one," said Mary a little breathlessly.

"Orv is deliberately flying so close," I decided out loud. "If he startles the people of the island, they'll come out of their houses to watch. Then Bo can photograph them."

Photographing Mr. Schnitzer seemed like a wonderful idea — especially since the *Miami Journal* hadn't been able to. Still, V.A.C.U.U.M.'s plan was to take pictures of the island without drawing unnecessary attention. As usual, however, Orv had grown overenthusiastic, and I didn't like it.

The De Havilland was now wobbling and coughing as if it had run out of everything all at once. A man in a bathing suit tore across the beach.

"Somebody better telephone the Coast Guard!" he panted. "That flying junkheap is about to fall apart!"

Many of the bathers had run for the telephone or their lives the first time Orv had circled above them, banking, clanking, and bumping. Now, after five minutes, the beach was absolutely deserted. Only a few umbrellas and chairs, abandoned in sheer panic, remained on the mile of sandy shoreline. Mary and I selected two matching chairs and sat down in the shade of a yellow umbrella.

Orv's air show lasted another few minutes. Then he leveled off, gunned the motor, and flew steadily back to the airstrip.

By afternoon, Bo had his pictures developed and printed. V.A.C.U.U.M. huddled in his darkroom as he pulled each print from the drier.

"Trees," said Orv, shuffling swiftly through the batch of twenty-five prints. "Trees . . . trees . . ."

"And more trees," said Horseshoes.

One photograph showed the large yacht moored to the dock at the gate. The other pictures were almost alike.

Mystery Island was entirely overgrown by dense, tropical jungle!

"It can't be," said Bo. "Even Germans don't live in trees any more."

The remark jarred loose understanding. "Camouflage!" I exclaimed. "The whole island is camouflaged! All those trees — I'll bet some of them are fakes. The roofs of the houses must be disguised by paint and nets and screens."

"It's got to be Cobra's headquarters," said Horseshoes.

For a long moment there was the tense silence of pent-up excitement. We all had the same thought. Orv expressed it.

"But those walls are twenty feet high," he said.

Walls or no walls, V.A.C.U.U.M. had to find out what was being so elaborately hidden on Mystery Island.

6

Twenty-four Hours Left

WHAT DEADLY STRIKE was Cobra planning against Miami unless the United States paid ten million dollars by June 15?

V.A.C.U.U.M. was convinced that the answer, or part of the answer, lay hidden under the dense camouflage of Mystery Island.

"We've got to find a way of getting inside those walls," I said carelessly, trying to cover up my unshakable belief that a bunch of teenagers hadn't a chance.

I didn't have to say anything about the danger. And I didn't mention the hard fact that Dad had enlisted our help for one good reason: to keep us from again upsetting the work of Mongoose. Everyone could see the calendar hanging on the wall of Bo's darkroom. In red crayon Bo had circled June 15.

June 15 was tomorrow.

At stake were the lives of more than a million innocent people dwelling in the Miami area. Compared to their safety, nothing else mattered — neither the danger we might encounter nor my dad's fear that we might somehow hamper his plans for stopping Cobra.

Less than twenty-four hours remained. V.A.C.U.U.M. had to act at once!

"I'm ready to pluck Cobra's fangs," announced Horseshoes, executing a neat dental yank on an imaginary snake. "But, please, somebody tell me how we get to Mystery Island without being seen? And how do we scale those walls?"

We sat in council on Bo's back porch. Reaching the island had seemed easy before we analyzed the difficulties. The putt-putt of an outboard motor would quickly give us away. Even the splash of a rowboat's oars would be heard. We might swim from Dadeland Beach, but the water would so tire us we wouldn't have the strength for the walls.

"We can stow away," I said.

"In what?" asked Horseshoes. "A string of seaweed?"

"In that big yacht of theirs," I said. "We can row out beyond the island tonight and ride the incoming tide silently, using oars to steer for the yacht. Then we can hide aboard."

I explained my idea. Perhaps we needn't explore Mystery Island after all. Cobra agents would undoubtedly use the yacht to carry out some part of the plot against Miami. We could stop them in the act.

It sounded beautiful, and it was: a beautiful, courageous plan — for somebody else.

The members of V.A.C.U.U.M. sagged gloomily in their seats. For lack of anything better to do, we drove to the waterfront to have another look at the island and the yacht tied at the dock.

The dock was empty.

Orv was the only one whose brain hadn't gone blank.

He said, "If we can find where the yacht is now, we might hide aboard her tonight. If she returns to Mystery Island, I know how we can get over the walls. I've been perfecting a climbing machine for two days."

We drove to Orv's house for a demonstration. He brought a foot-long tube from the pillbox. It seemed faintly familiar.

"This is the Davy-power pack from my fishing rod," he said. "I've made a few adjustments to control the speed of the cast and the winding mechanism, and I've substituted a stronger line."

Orv removed his right shoe and threw it ten yards. He aimed the handle and squeezed a button. The line zoomed out, and an adhesion cup at its tip struck the shoe. Orv squeezed another button. The shoe shot toward him as the line reeled in.

"Great," said Horseshoes. "You've knocked a barracuda cold in the Miami River. Now you've caught a shoe in the grass."

"How does a sawed-off fishing pole get us over the walls of Mystery Island?" asked Bo.

"The shoe moved toward me because it is lighter than I am," said Orv. "However, if the adhesion cup sticks to something that isn't movable, like a wall, *I'll* get reeled in."

He pointed the fishing pile handle at the highest point on the wall of his house and squeezed. The line cast out and the adhesion cup stuck.

He walked to the foot of the wall and squeezed again. Slowly he was lifted into the air.

He squeezed again and the handle cast, lowering him to the ground. Another squeeze raised the cup enough to break the adhesion. The line fed back into the handle.

"Man," said Bo. "Let's go find that big yacht."

The yacht could have put into any dock along the coast from Palm Beach to Key West, or into any of the canals between. We started the hunt at Key Biscayne marina, the docks nearest Mystery Island.

There we saw her. Although we stayed in the Rod to avoid notice, and viewed her from afar, we were sure she was the one. There aren't many sixty-foot Berton double cabin cruisers in Florida waters. They cost a hundred thousand dollars.

"Let's meet at Orv's house at eight o'clock tonight and then try to sneak aboard," I said.

Mary insisted upon joining the boarding party. We turned her down flat as a road map. The danger was too great for a girl, even for one who can defend herself in Japanese.

The dying sun had trimmed the treetops with an orange glow before I had delivered Mary, Horseshoes, and Bo to their homes. As I drove up to Orv's house, his dad waved and hurried toward us.

"I want you to go over to Mr. Vorhoose," Mr. Davy said to Orv. "Ask him whether he wants to enter the car meet at Reservoir City or the one at Orlando tomorrow," said Mr. Davy. "I must register Big Dog and make hotel reservations."

I backed the Rod onto the street obediently but without enthusiasm. It wasn't an assignment for two members of V.A.C.U.U.M.

"A fine thing!" I muttered. "We who are about to save Miami and foil Cobra — running errands! Messenger boys!"

"Don't fret," said Orv. "We can't do any counterspying till nightfall."

Mr. Vorhoose lived on Mindello Lane, the best street in Dade City. Behind his large white house was a canal where he moored his sleek, forty-foot sport fisherman.

We drove through the wrought-iron gateway and stopped by the garages. Parked inside were two cars which Orv's dad had rebuilt for him last year, a 1930 Packard and a 1931 Cadillac. I had decided that if I ever changed my mind about becoming a secret agent, I'd be a stock broker like Mr. Vorhoose and collect things nobody else could afford.

Orv rang the doorbell. A maid opened the door and summoned Mr. Vorhoose. He was a big, jolly man of fifty. He greeted Orv warmly and shook hands so long I thought he was trying to steal a finger. He liked Orv, all right.

They walked toward the Rod chatting like old buddies.

"Tell Dad to go ahead and make hotel reservations at both Orlando and Reservoir City," said Mr. Vorhoose. "I haven't decided upon which show yet. And remind him not to hook up a battery, hear? You know how I am. I must be the first to start a car when it looks like new again."

"I'll tell Dad," said Orv.

"Good," said Mr. Vorhoose And settling the matter with a storm of handshaking, he allowed Orv to escape into the Rod. Thus concluded V.A.C.U.U.M.'s duties as an errand service.

Or nearly so. After dinner Mom asked me to go to

Bromley's Drugstore and fetch two bottles of sleeping pills that Dr. Fenton had prescribed for her. Mom has always had trouble sleeping. Since Dad began stepping on Orv's alarm-rug twice a week, she has been getting less sleep than ever.

"I have important affairs pending with Orv, Bo, and Horseshoes tonight," I said. "Can't the pills wait, Mom?"

"I suppose so," she said, hurt. "I've enough for tonight. In the morning the drugstore will deliver."

I felt like a juvenile delinquent, and I was ashamed of myself. "I'll stop on the way to Orv's," I promised.

Mr. Bromley, the druggist, handed me the two bottles of sleeping pills along with some words of caution.

"Have your mother read the directions carefully," he warned. "The prescription is quite a bit stronger than the last one."

"Thank you," I said, tucking the bottles into my shirt pocket.

Mr. Bromley watched me, frowning in concern. "Three pills are enough to drop an elephant in his tracks," he remarked.

"I'll remember that if I'm ever in Africa," I thought, and thanked him again.

Bo and Horseshoes were already at Orv's house when I arrived, and we started for the Key Biscayne marina at ten minutes past eight. Keeping close to schedule was important. It gave us a sense of efficiency and bolstered our confidence.

I paid the toll at the Rickenbacker Causeway, which stretches across Biscayne Bay, connecting the island of Key Biscayne with the Miami mainland. Black water extended on both sides of us, silent, unknowable; and a strong sea breeze carried a damp whiff of the awful, limitless power of nature. I pressed the gas pedal, as if speed could protect us from fear.

We reached the marina and looked for the Berton double cabin cruiser. Out near the gasoline pumps and the snack shop she lay rocking gently at berth.

"Still there," whispered Horseshoes.

I couldn't tell whether he was glad or sorry.

We started walking across the parking lot toward the docks. Several boats were lighted. A phonograph record blared a dance tune, and girls were laughing.

It was going to be a long, long journey down the wooden pier to the big, darkened yacht.

7

Stowaways

MY LEGS TREMBLED as we moved toward the end of the pier where the big yacht was moored.

Along the way we halted to admire every boat. The little pauses were necessary. We had to pretend we were sightseeing in order to throw off suspicion.

A man came out of a sailboat. We stopped till he had left the pier. We resumed walking, keeping closer together.

We drew abreast of a boat from which music and giggles sounded, but nobody bothered with us. Another two boats were passed, and we reached the yacht from Mystery Island.

It lay at its berth, glistening under the string of overhead pier lights, silent and seemingly deserted.

Orv, Horseshoes, and I took a vote. We elected Bo to climb aboard the yacht and look around.

Bo slipped on deck. In one swift motion he ducked inside, which in the case of a seven-footer going through a four-foot door is something worthwhile to see.

We listened for one of his terrifying snarls. It would signal his encounter with a crew member and sound a general retreat. To our relief, he emerged grinning broadly. He waved all clear.

The rest of V.A.C.U.U.M. stepped aboard quite bravely. Pulling out pocket flashlights, we made ready to explore.

Horseshoes was posted as a lookout. Orv scampered aft to examine the engine room. Bo investigated the galley and master suite. I went fore.

The front of the yacht, I discovered, was rather out of the ordinary. For one thing, there were no bunks in the sleeping area, only drums of diesel fuel. For another thing, opposite the head was a large closet that contained more medicine bottles than Mr. Bromley's drugstore.

We gathered in the salon to swap notes.

"Nothing is in the master suite but refrigerators," said Bo. "They're packed with enough food to give everybody in China heartburn."

"The engines are big enough to drive a battleship," said Orv. "And those fuel tanks! I'll bet this ship can cruise halfway around the world."

"All the way around," I corrected. "Up front is more fuel — at least a six-month's supply."

"We should tell Ken's dad what we've found," said Orv. "I'm scared. Let's get out of here."

"The sooner the better," I agreed.

"Too late," said Horseshoes over by the window. "Lie down!"

We dropped without arguing. "What — ?" I asked.

"Two men got out of a parked car," said Horseshoes. "They must have been sitting there all the time!"

"Which way are they walking?" asked Bo.

"The wrong way," replied Horseshoes.

He didn't have to say more. We could hear their footsteps on the pier now, growing louder. They stopped right by us, whispering. Suddenly headlights flashed over the yacht. The footsteps quickly started again, as though the two men had been frightened off.

"What's happening?" inquired Bo.

"A car drove into the parking lot," reported Horseshoes, peeking around a curtain. "Three men are getting out . . . and . . . here we go again!"

"What about the first two men?" asked Orv from the floor.

"They were a false alarm," replied Horseshoes. "They're admiring a sailboat."

The planks of the dock squeaked and rumbled as the three new arrivals approached.

Horseshoes went winging by, moaning something which sounded like, "Take cover!"

We didn't pause to consider our reputation as spies or counterspies. In fact, we didn't consider anything but our necks. We tumbled toward the front of the yacht in pie-eyed flight from discovery.

By virtue of his quick start, Horseshoes shot into an early lead. Bo overtook him passing the medicine closet. At the fuel drums, V.A.C.U.U.M. piled up like duckpins.

"We've had it!" groaned Orv, unable to squeeze past Horseshoes, who was wiggling between drums.

I grabbed Orv by the collar. "In here!" I said.

We flopped into the medicine closet. I barely had shut the door when footfalls clumped on the rear deck. All any of us could do now was pray and breathe seldom.

Muffled orders, a scattering of steps, and presently the engines throbbed. The yacht traveled smoothly through the quiet harbor waters and speeded up as it struck waves. We were in Biscayne Bay.

I felt it safe to move. I raised my right foot, which had fallen across Orv's neck, and we shifted gingerly into comfortable positions. As the yacht rolled and pitched, I heard the two bottles of sleeping pills in my shirt pocket clinking together.

In the current state of my health, which was weak with terror, I foresaw the bottles knocking against each

other till they broke, and a sharp piece of glass bearing the label, "Take Two Before Retiring," plunging into my heart.

I ran my fingers along the shelf by Orv's leg. The last holes on the left were empty and the correct size. I fitted Mom's two bottles into them for safekeeping.

From the deck above the voices of the three men carried faintly down to the closet. They spoke in a foreign language, and I made nothing of what they said.

After twenty minutes the engines slowed, reversed, and idled. The yacht drifted a moment and bumped gently against a dock. We had arrived, somewhere. . . .

Orv and I listened to the three men leaving. Their departure was a relief in more ways than one. I'd been hearing them walk back and forth so long my brain was footsore. A distant creaking, like a heavy gate or door swinging open and shut, mingled with the fading voices and footfalls. Then the night was still.

Orv and I played it safe. We stayed in the closet another couple of minutes. We heard nothing. Cautiously I opened the door and peeped out. On my right was the darkened salon. I should have peeped to my left. All at once the yacht heaved and the darkness lit up like a barn burning.

When I awoke Bo was leaning over me.

"Are you all right?" he asked fearfully.

"My head feels loose," I answered. "What happened?"

"I mistook you for a Cobra agent," Bo apologized. "Why didn't you tell me you and Orv hid in the closet?"

"It's the salt air," I thought. "It's frazzled him."

"Lucky for you Bo didn't have more punching room," said Horseshoes.

"That's a comfort," I said, touching the right side of my jaw. It was swollen out to there. "Where are we?"

"Mystery Island," said Orv.

8

Lion Below

THE WALLS of Mystery Island towered less than thirty feet away.

Aboard the yacht the men of V.A.C.U.U.M. stared at the mass of stone and heard duty calling.

Over the top, brave lads! Strangle the viper in its den!

Ah, the opportunity for fame undying! It was not the thanks of a grateful nation, however, which filled our heads. It was self-preservation. Those walls looked close enough.

An idea of mine, to pirate the yacht and sail her to safe harbor, had a moment of glory. But Orv reported that the crew had snatched the ignition key.

Three courses of action, then, lay open. V.A.C.-U.U.M. could:

1. Remain in hiding and trust that the yacht's outbound voyage was back to Key Biscayne and not to Australia or Egypt.

2. Behave as daring counterspies should and investigate the island.

3. Chuck the heroics and swim for home.

A secret ballot would have unanimously declared for the swim. No one, however, had the decency to speak out and confess he loved his hide more than duty. So after a period of hemming and hawing, sidelong glances, feet shifting, and knuckle cracking, we voted for a show of nerve. Bo led us ashore.

We halted in front of the gate's huge, steel-plated doors.

"No chance of breaking them down," said Orv. "Besides, they're probably wired with more alarms than a firehouse."

So we put our faith in V.A.C.U.U.M.'s secret weapon — Orv's wonderful Davy-powered fishing rod handle. Horseshoes had dubbed it the Wall Walker, but he foresaw broader fields of conquest. It would, he said, revolutionize the sport of mountain climbing. It needed but a catchy trade name. He offered Pikes Peak's Peachy Peril Preventer and Everyman's Aid to Alpine Ascension as starters.

Bo volunteered to be first up the wall. We at once yielded him the honor. He picked his way over the narrow ledge of coral which separated the wall from the black waters of the bay.

After traveling some twenty feet, he stopped, aimed, and squeezed. The adhesion cup shot up and took hold. A squeeze of the retractor button and Bo, all two hundred and forty pounds of him, zoomed after the cup. He reached one arm up and hauled himself the last foot to the top. Then he released the adhesion cup, retracted the fishing line, and tossed me the Wall Walker.

I was still dizzy from the clout on the chin Bo had delivered by accident. I must have wobbled like a penguin, because Orv asked if I were okay.

"I'm dandy," I answered, wishing I were a lot dizzier so that I couldn't think about what we were doing.

I made a lucky shot and scrambled to the top unassisted. Orv landed the adhesion cup too low on the wall and had to be helped the rest of the way. Horseshoes escaped disaster by the seat of his pants. He squeezed the retractor button too hard and sailed over our heads. Bo snagged him by the bottom and fielded him like a line drive.

"Thanks," gasped Horseshoes. "I thought I was a goner."

A long fall wasn't all Bo had saved him from. Horseshoes had scarcely sat down when we heard a strange, heavy breathing and the rattle of a chain dragging.

Into the patch of moonlight directly below us padded a full grown lion.

"How high can a lion jump?" inquired Horseshoes.

"We are about to find out," said Orv in a small voice.

The king of beasts did not, however, show off his jumping ability. Perhaps in the past he had learned the impossibility of gobbling intruders off the wall. He contented himself with training his lively yellow eyes on us and swishing his tail as if he were brushing away table crumbs before the meat dish. He possessed a very fine set of teeth, which he suddenly revealed. The shaggy jaws opened wide as a tunnel, and an earthquaking roar issued forth.

"If we took another vote right now, I'd be in favor of swimming for home," said Horseshoes.

"What about using the Wall Walker, Orv?" asked Bo. "It knocked a barracuda cold at fifty feet."

"I can't be sure," answered Orv. "It might knock him silly for a while. But even a silly lion is no laughing matter."

We held a hurried council on the subject of retreat. While we whispered, we kept our eyes fixed on the big cat. He paced silently at the end of his chain, back and forth, wasting not a muscle-twitch in looking up. He knew. If we forsook our perch, he could have us all in one bound and a swipe of a paw.

"Why not put him to sleep?" I said.

I had reached into my pocket before I remembered. My mom's sleeping pills were still aboard the yacht.

"That old lion doesn't look like he'd go for a bedtime story," said Horseshoes. "You're still punchy from Bo's right cross."

"We can drug him," I said. "I left my mother's sleeping pills in the medicine closet aboard the yacht."

"Was that what you put on the shelf by my leg?" asked Orv.

"I was afraid the bottles might break in my pocket," I said. "Look, the yacht is provisioned for a getaway to any port in the seven seas. Stored on board must be some kind of food lions like. Stuff the pills into a couple of pounds of goodies and presto! One snoring pussy-cat!"

It sounded as easy as going to bed. Even Horseshoes admitted it was worth an attempt.

Because I was still dizzy, Orv insisted upon fetching the bottles in my place. Bo went with him to bring back some lion food.

Horseshoes and I kept our spirits up by making faces at Mr. Lion. Our cheek muscles ached by the time Orv and Bo reappeared on deck.

Orv tapped his pocket to show me the pills were now in V.A.C.U.U.M.'s possession. Bo carried a large cardboard box.

"Chopped meat — *hamburgers!*" Bo whispered gleefully upon regaining the top of the wall. He set the box down and helped Orv up.

We formed a production line. Orv took out six pills and handed them to Bo, who sank them into a burger ball. We'd decided that a small dose of six pills would be about right. More than six, and the lion would sniff and turn up his nose.

Bo passed the burger ball, now a fully loaded burger bomb, to Horseshoes.

Although Bo can throw a baseball from first base to Georgia, the choice of a pitcher had fallen upon Horseshoes. For the job at hand, a delicate touch was necessary.

"Wait till he opens his mouth," I coached. "Shoot for his throat."

"I'll part his tonsils," vowed Horseshoes.

Below, Mr. Lion couldn't have cared less for our schemes. Head down, he paced back and forth with the air of a king working up an appetite.

"Here kitty, kitty. Here kitty," crooned Horseshoes.

The lion ignored the invitation to look up. Stronger measures were called for.

"I'll give him a dose of the Wall Walker at full power," whispered Orv. "Ready?"

Horseshoes nodded.

Orv aimed and squeezed.

The adhesion cup socked Mr. Lion in the rump and bowled him over. He leaped up in a surge of scrambling legs. His mouth opened wide for the roar of roars.

Horseshoes pitched a ringer.

The burger bomb on the way down met the roar on the way up. The collision produced a ferocious burp. Mr. Lion looked startled. He licked his chops questioningly.

Bo had another burger bomb ready. Horseshoes waved the meat and coaxed. Mr. Lion watched him, but with close-mouthed interest.

We couldn't use the Wall Walker again. It would rouse Mr. Lion when we were trying to put him to sleep. Those jaws would open in a yawn eventually. We had to sweat it out.

Five long minutes stretched into ten before the great black mane shook and the first yawn laid the white fangs bare. Horseshoes had to be fast. He let one go from the hip. The huge jaws snapped shut and the yellow eyes blinked in surprise.

"Two for two!" said Horseshoes. "I'm hot tonight!"

Orv replaced the empty pill bottle in his pocket. I

motioned him to seed the next burger bomb with all the pills in Mom's other bottle. We had been perched atop the walls too long already.

Bo doubled the size of the burger bomb to hold all twelve pills. Horseshoes juggled this de luxe serving in his hand, getting the feel.

Mr. Lion stopped pacing. He was watching Horseshoes closely.

"Nice kitty," whispered Horseshoes. "Say Ahhhh."

The lion was either highly intelligent or plain sleepy. Forthwith he gave a mighty yawn, and Horseshoes dropped the twelve-pill blockbuster squarely between his fangs.

"Now we wait," I thought. "And if Mr. Lion doesn't flop over with his feet in the air, V.A.C.U.U.M. takes to the water."

I sat on the wall feeling good about V.A.C.U.U.M.'s performance, regardless of whether Mr. Lion allowed us to slip by. We hadn't lost our nerve. We had met the emergency coolly and cleverly in the best tradition of undercover agents. Two bottles of sleeping pills had never been more imaginatively used in all the history of spying.

"Dad will be proud of us," I thought confidently.

I had forgotten about Dad's warning against overconfidence. When an agent grows overconfident, Dad says, he drops his guard. When he does that, some unpleasant surprise steals up and knocks him and his plans into a pickle barrel.

Dad was right, as usual.

I was sitting on the wall in a glow when I noticed Orv. He put the second empty bottle into his pocket and removed another bottle. He snapped off the cap and poured the pills onto the palm of his hand. Bo scooped them up and stuffed them into a double helping of hamburger.

I glanced away to check on Mr. Lion. It was a moment before I realized what I'd just seen.

9

The Mystery Bottle

BEFORE I COULD DO ANYTHING, Horseshoes had pitched another ringer. The pills from the third bottle were beyond recovery, being on course somewhere between Mr. Lion's fangs and belly.

My alarm was with numbers. I had put two bottles of pills on the shelf in the medicine closet of the yacht. Orv had brought out *three*.

Bo and Horseshoes relayed my frantic whispers to Orv. The three empty bottles were passed to me.

They were ordinary K-5 snap cap bottles, the kind druggists use to fill all sorts of prescriptions. Two of them had Mr. Bromley's labels, on which were type-written my mother's name and address, and the directions. The third bottle was without a label.

I couldn't blame Orv for the mistake. It was dark, the bottles were the same size and shape, and I hadn't told him how many I'd left aboard.

Fortunately, he did recall the order in which he had used the bottles. The first two bottles emptied were Mom's sleeping pills.

That left the big question. What kind of pills were in the third bottle?

We watched Mr. Lion for a clue.

He was acting like an alley cat that has just been belted with a flying shoe. His legs buckled, his head rolled, and his eyes were having fits in slow motion. Three sleeping pills, Mr. Bromley had warned me, would stop an elephant in his tracks. The lion had devoured twenty-four!

Sleepy as eight elephants, the lion staggered a few steps, yawned, and collapsed. His eyes danced a dragging fox-trot together and slammed closed.

"Go to sleep," murmured Horseshoes, weaving his hands like a wizard casting an enchantment. "Go--oooo to slee-eeppp, you big, bad pussycat."

The lion lay like a stone among the sweet peas.

"He doesn't hear you," said Bo. "He's down for the count."

"Make me know it," requested Horseshoes. He worked some hamburger into a ball. "Here," he said, handing

the meatball to Bo. "Bean him between the eyes, and give it all you have."

Bo wound up. I felt almost sorry for the poor, unsuspecting lion. Suddenly Bo stopped, his arm frozen in mid-delivery.

Mr. Lion had stirred. His eyes remained shut tight. But his tongue ran over his jaws in a strange way.

The flicking tongue disappeared. The eyes jolted open.

"The mystery pills are taking effect," I thought.

The shaggy head lifted. The yellow eyes turned in our direction and fixed on a spot of the wall to our left. This was no big pussycat staring, but a jungle killer taut with hatred.

Belly pressed to the ground, he began to glide forward. His eyes were bright with the glitter of an animal sighting prey.

No lion in a zoo or circus ever behaved like this one. He wasn't pacing or growling. Every sinew of him was the deadly hunter.

"If I didn't know it was impossible, I'd swear he sees something on this wall we don't," said Horseshoes.

Bo upended the cardboard box. He shook out the remains of the hamburger meat. The lion ignored it.

It was spooky.

"He should be snoring in his tracks," I said.

"Maybe he's sleepwalking," said Horseshoes.

The lion inched toward the wall, stalking. He stopped, frozen with a paw in midair, as if his prey had given a sign of fleeing. Then he advanced again.

It happened suddenly. In one mighty spring, he hurled himself against a spot close to the empty wall on our left. Snarling, paws striking, he twisted and thrashed upon the ground. He was making a kill.

I watched spellbound. I could almost see a zebra being torn apart.

The struggle ceased. The lion rose. Leaning as if weighted by a carcass in his jaws, he moved backward. Some twenty feet from the wall he lay down. His jaw ripped and chewed as he ate great chunks of nothing.

V.A.C.U.U.M. didn't waste time on a conference. We all knew from the sound of our knees which side of the wall we wanted to go down.

Orv led off. The moment his feet touched the coral ledge outside the wall, he threw the Wall Walker to Bo.

I heard a swish and rustle of foliage. A man's voice commanded, "Hold it right there!"

My heart skipped more beats than a monkey band. "At least Orv will get away," I thought.

The creak of the steel gate opening informed me I was wrong.

Four men in uniform strode into the patch of moonlight at the base of the wall. They had rifles.

"Get down," one of the men ordered.

We got down. The Wall Walker was taken from Bo at gunpoint.

"You can put the guns away, officers," said Horseshoes. "It's hazing week. You know, schoolboy stuff."

None of the men said a word.

"We're being initiated into a secret high school society," said Horseshoes, as though it were as plain as the nose on your face. "We have to get inside the walls or we don't get inside the society."

"This is the fourteenth of June," said one of the men. "School is over for the summer."

"We go to summer school," replied Horseshoes in despair over such ignorance.

Orv was brought inside the walls by two burly guards, and the four founding fathers of V.A.C.U.U.M. were searched. When our pockets were unloaded, we were told to march.

The guards jabbed us with their guns to keep us on the path. Occasional splashes of moonlight relieved the unnatural darkness, but most of the journey was made in blackest black.

Above our heads stretched a vast screen roof. It was strewn with leaves and branches that concealed the low buildings which squatted as dim, vague shapes to our left and right. The screens ended wherever the natural vegetation grew thickly and no man-made objects stood.

Then we saw the moon and the stars for ten or twenty feet before the screening blotted out the sky again.

We had read Bo's aerial photographs correctly. The island was camouflaged like a battlefield command post!

After walking without benefit of flashlight for three or four minutes, we were ordered to halt.

In front of us was a rambling, one-story house. A single yellow bulb lit the heavy wood door. One of the guards went inside.

Horseshoes leaned to me and whispered, "We could threaten them with Mr. Wolovski."

Mr. Wolovski was our principal. "Threaten them with Mr. Bates," I replied. Mr. Bates was chairman of the School Board.

Before Horseshoes could threaten them with either, the guard reappeared at the door. He thumbed us inside.

We filed through the door, pushed aside a heavy curtain, and entered a brightly lighted foyer.

"Keep walking," the guard commanded.

We passed into a small green room. The door was shut behind us and locked.

We saw it immediately, for there was nothing else in the green room but a rug, six chairs, and a side table.

Upon the table, fixed in a position of striking — its poison fangs extended and its hood enlarged — was a statue of a cobra.

10

Captured

A voice spoke from the mouth of the cobra.

"Please sit down. Make yourself at home."

It was impossible for anyone but a midget or a bellboy to make himself at home in the green room. It was not much larger than an elevator.

We sat down stiffly. An instant later I shot to my feet. The cobra seemed alive. It was rising . . .

So was the door. The doorknob rose higher and higher.

I felt a moment of weightlessness before I realized neither the statue nor the door was moving.

The floor was lowering. The green room *was* an elevator.

The table which supported the statue remained fixed

against the wall as silently and steadily V.A.C.U.U.M. sank below it and the door. After we had descended ten or twelve feet, our journey stopped with a mild bump. Opposite us was another door. After a few minutes, it swung open.

"Come in," a voice said.

We followed Bo into an underground room. The walls were lined with TV screens. Below the screens were steel panels crowded with dials, buttons, levers, gauges, and knobs. The place looked like the control center for steering the earth.

In the middle of the room was an elevated chair, high-backed as a throne. It was topped by a huge bronze statue of a cobra. In front of it stood a desk.

A fat man with a pointed beard sat on the throne. He beckoned us close.

"I cannot bid you welcome," he said. "We do not encourage visitors to our island. As you can see, we are not in the tourist business."

He continued beckoning till we were lined up in front of his desk. The way he looked at the four of us struck me as odd. He should have stared at Bo, for it isn't every night that a boy seven feet tall walks into your office. However, he regarded us equally, as if he were afraid of revealing a special interest in one.

"My name is Hans Schnitzer," he said, leaning back and

tapping his fingertips together. "You will, please, tell me your names."

"Jeremiah Kates," said Horseshoes.

"Booker T. Johnson," said Bo.

"Orville H. Davy," said Orv.

"Kenneth Mullins," I said.

Mr. Schnitzer, I thought, had taken his eyes from me too quickly.

He picked up the Wall Walker and examined it with an air of amusement. On his desk lay the other things the guards had taken from us — the stuff we'd had in our pockets and the three empty pill bottles.

"You may take your belongings — except this," he said, tapping the Wall Walker against his palm.

We leaned over the desk. Bo's huge hands were within grasp of the pudgy throat.

Mr. Schnitzer saw his danger and pressed a red button. A trap door sprung open behind the throne. Three guards, guns drawn, were lifted into the room.

Mr. Schnitzer chuckled and adopted a fatherly tone. He asked who had invented the Wall Walker. Being told, he declared Orv to be the greatest boy wonder since Mozart.

"He's laying it on pretty thick," I thought.

Mr. Schnitzer rapped the Wall Walker upon the desk. "But you did not come here to show me this clever toy," he said. "Now, why did you come, please?"

Horseshoes said that we'd swum over from Dadeland Beach on a dare.

Mr. Schnitzer received the story with a look of disappointment. He pushed a yellow button on his desk. A TV screen flashed on. We saw ourselves sneaking out of the yacht.

Mr. Schnitzer pushed another button. Another TV set flickered on. The screen seemed blank. Then Orv's World War I De Havilland shuddered into view. It swooped low, and Mr. Schnitzer flipped a switch. The TV tape held upon a stop-action close-up of Bo and Orv in the cockpits.

"My young friends," said Mr. Schnitzer, turning off the TV sets. "Suppose you tell me the truth."

"We're thieves," I said. "Call the police."

Again Mr. Schnitzer chuckled, a sound as jolly as an ax being sharpened.

"The police will come," he said. "We expect them. But when they come, we shall be gone."

He pushed two buttons, and two TV screens lighted. One showed an airplane set upon end, like a space rocket upon a launching pad. The other showed a submarine in an underground chamber.

"We have been aware that both your local and federal police have been observing the island for more than a year," he said. "In other countries, they would have searched the island. Not in America. Here we are quite safe till we break a law. So we have been very, very careful."

Mr. Schnitzer turned off the two television screens. "Now come, boys," he said, coaxingly. "I have been open and honest with you. Speak to me in kind. Who sent you?"

We remained silent. Mr. Schnitzer fought to control his temper. He chuckled his chuckle.

"In two hours and nine minutes it will be the fifteenth day of June," he said. "You know that unless your President meets Cobra's demands for ten million dollars, the people of Miami will suffer. It will be a fate more terrible than an atomic bombing."

"Ten million dollars won't even give you a profit," said Orv. "Changing this island into a Cobra fortress must have cost that much!"

"You speak well," said Mr. Schnitzer. "The submarine pen alone cost nearly a million dollars."

"The President of the United States doesn't do business with criminals," said Orv quietly. "He won't pay Cobra a cent."

"You are quite right, young man," said Mr. Schnitzer. "Your President won't pay ten million because he does not believe we can destroy the people of Miami. The Japanese did not believe you Americans had an atomic bomb . . ."

Mr. Schnitzer sighed, as if it were a strain and a nuisance for him to be explaining such matters to children.

"Today your President will pay nothing. He thinks we are bluffing. Tomorrow — ach! Tomorrow, Miami will be the diaster center of the world. Then he will see how useless it is to be stubborn. He will pay — not ten million dollars, but *one hundred million!*"

Mr. Schnitzer picked up the empty, unmarked pill bottle from his desk. He rubbed it between his fat hands.

"My poor, poor lion," he said sorrowfully. "An innocent victim of man's greed. Most unfortunate."

"What kind of pills were in that bottle?" said Orv.

"I shall tell you," replied Mr. Schnitzer.

He stared beyond us for an instant, as if glimpsing a future in which Cobra was all-powerful.

"In the bottle," he said, "were memory pills."

I recalled how the lion, after eating a bottle of the pills, had slain and devoured a prey that wasn't there. I didn't understand what the pill did. I had only a feeling about it, but the feeling was enough to make my skin crawl.

For some reason, Mr. Schnitzer was now pleased to boast of Cobra's might. Perhaps it was because we were his prisoners; we could do nothing with the information. At any rate, he spoke for ten minutes. He told us the whole history of Cobra's plot against Miami.

Cobra, he said, had been formed right after World War II by three escaped war criminals. Over the years, Cobra had grown in numbers, cunning, and wealth; and as it grew, it pressed the search for new and better weapons. Ten years ago the first memory pill was developed.

The drug was too weak, however. An entire pill was required to affect one person. The experiments continued.

It was a bottle of these early pills, Mr. Schnitzer explained, which we had unknowingly fed the lion.

"We have made progress," said Schnitzer. "The cost has been great. But now we have the drug in the form of a powder, not a pill. Our entire supply would not fill a woman's purse, and yet it is enough. One dose no larger than a grain of salt will infect a thousand people."

"Will the people die?" I heard myself ask.

"Oh, no," said Mr. Schnitzer. "They will simply lose the use of all five senses for twenty-four hours."

"But how will they move around?" asked Horseshoes. "They won't be able to see, hear, feel, taste, or smell. They'll be paralyzed!"

"You are quite right — but only in a way," said Mr. Schnitzer. "Although blind, they will see; although deaf, they will hear. They will taste, feel, smell. Those who work will go to their jobs. Mothers will cook meals which children will eat — or so they will think."

He was talking riddles. We weren't sure whether he was making fun of us. So we stood there in grim silence, unwilling to ask more questions.

"You do not believe me?" he said. "You do not believe that a man who cannot see can drive a car?"

"No," said Orv.

"You do not believe," he said, "because I have not told you everything. The drug deadens the senses, yes. But that is only half of what it does."

He drew a long luxurious breath.

"The drug," he continued, "replaces the world outside with the inward world, the world of memory. The eyes see; but what they see is the past. Once drugged, the victim lives again all that has happened to him during the past twenty-four hours."

I thought again of the lion and shivered. We had drugged him by accident, and he had attacked and eaten something that existed only in his memory.

"Tomorrow," I thought, "a million people will move about Miami. Each will be closed in by the world of his memory!"

I saw a million people living again every detail of the previous twenty-four hours as if those hours were happening for the first time. They would feel, see, taste, smell, and hear all the details as real experience rather than as memory.

"Can you imagine a city filled with a million people and each acting separately, each unable to see or feel anyone else?" asked Mr. Schnitzer. "You cannot? Well, then, permit me to describe the fate of two men — any two men. I shall call them Mr. Jones and Mr. Smith."

I listened with mounting horror as he spoke. His words drew a picture of Mr. Jones and Mr. Smith at lunch tomorrow in a Miami restaurant. I saw the two men clearly in my mind.

Mr. Jones suddenly stopped eating, for the drug had taken control of him. His hands went up and gripped a steering wheel that wasn't there, because twenty-four hours earlier he had driven his car to the hardware store.

At the next table Mr. Smith suddenly believed he was walking down Flagler Street. He got up and walked. Unable to see, he bumped into Mr. Jones. Both men fell to the floor. Neither felt the fall or knew it had happened. Mr. Smith's legs continued to move; he still believed he was walking down Flagler Street. Mr. Jones's arms were still curved in front of him; he had not yet reached the hardware store, and he still believed he was seated behind the wheel of his car.

Mr. Schnitzer finished the description. He regarded our expressions of horror with amusement.

Orv was the first to recover himself.

"How do you expect to make the people of Miami eat the drug?" he demanded.

"They will drink it," declared Mr. Schnitzer. "Cobra agents right now are working in the six dairies which supply Miami. By nine o'clock tomorrow morning, every person who has drunk milk from a glass, or with coffee or cereal, will begin to relive his last twenty-four hours."

11

Rainbow to the Rescue

ALL AT ONCE the Cobra control center seemed like a safe place to be.

If somehow we escaped to Miami, we might wish we had remained on the island.

By noon tomorrow, Miami would be a madhouse.

Mr. Schnitzer read the horror on our faces.

"I have been frank with you," he said. "Now, please, why have you come?"

Orv, Bo, Horseshoes, and I were too shocked to say a word.

"Very well," said Mr. Schnitzer. "I give you until the sun rises to think over the matter. If you do not talk then, I shall make you talk. Believe me, my young friends, I have methods."

He raised one hand above his shoulder and snapped his fingers. "Take them to the blockhouse."

The three armed guards behind him herded us into the green elevator-room. We rode to the surface meek as lambs. After a short march outside, we were ordered into a small, square building with a gravel roof.

I stepped to the only window and looked out through the steel bars. The overhead screen stopped to allow several big palms to rise upward freely. A large patch of sky showed between the tall trunks, and I saw storm clouds moving rapidly below the stars.

One of the guards entered the room with us. He flipped on the yellow ceiling light, pulled a shade over the window, and locked the door.

The room was almost bare. A three-legged stool lay overturned in a corner. A double bunk bed stood against the wall opposite the window.

The guard ordered us into the bunks. Orv and I shared the lower. Bo and Horseshoes climbed on top.

"You can talk, but keep your voices low," said the guard, pulling the stool over to the window. He sat down with his back to the wall, his gun flat across his thighs. "And don't move off those blankets."

We lay stiff with fright. I wished someone would say something funny. But even Horseshoes was at a loss for a joke.

We all knew we'd have to tell Mr. Schnitzer the truth — that we were V.A.C.U.U.M., a name the enemies of America would someday learn to fear. If we lied, he'd get the truth out of us by drugs or torture or something.

Why he hadn't forced the truth from us immediately puzzled me.

"I wonder why Mr. Schnitzer is *really* keeping us cooped up," I whispered to Orv.

Orv wasn't listening. He was looking at the tiny compass he kept on the chain of his pocket flashlight.

"The window faces due east," he whispered.

That piece of information seemed outstandingly useless at first. Then I understood. If we managed to break out of the blockhouse, we'd have our bearings despite the darkness. The gate in the wall faced the mainland, due west.

"Orv hasn't stopped thinking," I said to myself reproachfully. Swallowing my fear, I set myself to planning an escape.

I dreamed up several nifty schemes. Each had a shortcoming. The guard always blew our heads off before we reached the door.

So the first step was to silence the guard. I rolled on my side and measured the distance from the bunk to him with my eyes. Four strides would cover the distance.

I rehearsed the route over and over, like a broad jumper learning the runway. If ever the guard put down his gun for a moment, I was ready to charge him.

The guard changed at midnight. The new man locked the door and sat down. He crossed his legs and laid the barrel of his rifle over his raised knee. The muzzle pointed directly at me, as if the metal tipped to danger like a divining rod to hidden water.

I made a great pose of studying my watch. The sweep hand seemed to travel haltingly. Every minute passed like three.

The guard changed on the hour. Each man looked bigger, meaner, and more alert than the man he replaced.

At three o'clock in the morning I thought: "The milk is being put on the delivery trucks at the dairies."

A little after four o'clock a storm broke. I prayed it slowed up the milk trucks.

Rain fell steadily until twenty minutes before six. Fifteen minutes later the sky cleared, and the early rays of dawn edged the window shade.

The guard switched off the light and raised the shade. He held his rifle low, at his hip, and leaned an elbow on the sill and peered up into the sky.

He had turned his back to the room before I realized I had missed my chance. A knock sounded on the door, and a voice said gruffly, "Number Nine relieving Number Four."

Number Four unlocked the door and gave Number Nine the key.

"There's a rainbow. Have a look," said Number Four. He nodded toward us. "They're asleep."

I guessed that Orv, Bo, and Horseshoes were doing what I was doing, faking sleep and observing the guards through slitted lashes.

Number Four departed, and Number Nine locked the door after him. He stood in the center of the floor and eyed us for a moment. Then, satisfied, he walked to the window. He leaned his rifle against the wall by his right leg and stared up into the sky.

I didn't miss my chance again. I was off the bunk in a flash. I hit on my left foot, found my balance, and shot forward. Fists cocked, I'd taken two strides when something walloped me and sent me flying across the room.

It was Bo's shoulder. "Next time," I thought, "V.A.C.U.U.M. better coordinate its plan of attack."

I had just regained my feet when Bo knocked me down again — with the guard.

"He's out cold," I whispered, rolling the unconscious man off me.

After a flurry of hand signals, we got busy. Bo and I tore up the sheets and bound and gagged the guard. Orv stripped off his copper-colored uniform. Horseshoes, who was nearest the guard's size, donned each piece of clothing as Orv tossed it to him.

Our teamwork was nearly perfect. The only delay occurred when I accidentally tied Orv's wrist under the gag as he was unbuttoning the guard's collar.

The guard was still out when Bo and I carried him across the floor. We laid him on the lower bunk.

"Let's see how you look," Orv said to Horseshoes.

Horseshoes flung his arms wide and turned slowly around for all to admire his uniform.

"Splendid," said Bo. "With a bucket over your head you'd even fool Mr. Schnitzer."

"It itches," said Horseshoes. "I'm in torture."

"Scratch and let's go," said Orv.

Horseshoes scratched, picked up the rifle, and unlocked the door. He stuck his head out.

"It's dark on this side," he said nervously.

Bo pushed him out. I brought up the rear and carefully closed the door behind me. Time, which had crawled like a snail inside the blockhouse, was now speeding on rabbit's feet. Any minute Mr. Schnitzer might decide it was sunrise and summon us to explain why we had come.

We struck out due west toward the gate. The overhead screens blocked the feeble rays of dawn, and we easily stayed in the shadows.

We had covered about two hundred yards when we took council behind a hedge of hibiscus bushes. Orv was positive the gate was less than fifty yards ahead.

"How are we going to get over the wall if the gate is closed?" Horseshoes whispered anxiously.

The question went unanswered. For at that instant we

heard talking. We crouched behind the hibiscus bushes and peeped through the leaves.

A dozen men in street clothes were passing within two feet of us. They carried large crates and grumbled at the burden. The sharp scuff of their shoes indicated they walked upon a paved path — probably the one we had used last night, the one that led to the gate.

"They're packed and preparing to quit the island," I thought as the last man passed me, struggling and grunting.

Orv prodded an elbow into my ribs. Bo and Horseshoes were already creeping along the bushes after the parade of men. I followed on hands and knees.

We clung to cover, and when there was none, squirmed on our bellies. In this manner we traveled another fifty yards. Abruptly everything around us brightened, as if the sun had risen above the horizon. I looked up. The screening had ended. Daylight gilded the top of the wall!

By straining my neck around a coconut palm, I spied the gate. It was ajar.

"Ten more yards," Orv whispered, "and we're free."

"It's going to be the longest ten yards of our lives," I replied.

From beyond the wall came noises of activity and freedom. The crates thudding upon the wood dock mingled with the steady lap and splatter of the waves against the coral rock.

As though of one mind, Orv, Bo, Horseshoes, and I began to strip for the swim to the mainland. I had removed my shoes when the men returned through the gate.

They trooped by us, some of them so close I could have rapped their ankles. We remained pressed to the ground till their footfalls and voices drifted away. Then we looked up and saw a miracle. The gate had been left open.

Without warning, Horseshoes took it into his head to play scout. He stole forward, clutching the rifle like a housewife about to attack the porch steps with a broom.

Bo rose up and waved wildly in an attempt to stop him. But Horseshoes, his back to us, continued to within a foot of the steel doors.

At that point a man in a tan business suit strolled around a door. He nearly bumped into Horseshoes. For a startled second they gaped at each other, nose to nose.

Then Horseshoes snapped, "Schnitzer wants the gate open. Number Ten is fetching some stuff from the submarine that must be stored aboard the yacht."

It was a beautiful, nervy bit of bluff, and in his copper-colored uniform Horseshoes might have succeeded. But, alas, he wore only the shirt. The boots and pants he had left behind in the bushes.

The man's right hand darted into his jacket and came out with a pistol. Horseshoes, leaping backward, stumbled as it discharged.

The rifle in Horseshoes' hands went off as he danced around for balance. The man clutched his chest and toppled to the ground.

The two shots had given V.A.C.U.U.M. away. In half a minute every guard on the island would be racing to the gate.

12

Escape

THE MAN in the tan suit had fallen forward in front of the open gate doors. His right hand, which had clutched his chest, was pinned awkwardly beneath him.

Horseshoes swayed back on his heels, pale and limp. His eyes, round with disbelief, were fixed upon the death-like figure.

Bo bounded up. He tucked Horseshoes under his arm like a loaf of French bread and sped through the gate. Orv and I reached the dock a stride behind.

The big yacht lolled at her moorings. Bo veered sharply, for two men in white were swabbing her rear deck. At the sight of V.A.C.U.U.M. escaping, they dropped their mops and started shouting.

Tied to the dock behind the yacht was a fisherman with a single outboard motor. It lay low in the water, and I didn't see it till Bo dropped the dazed Horseshoes onto the rear seat.

After that it was just like undocking Horseshoes' own runabout at high speed. Bo cast off in front and I did the same with the stern line. As we hopped aboard, Orv had the engine running full blast. We shot away from the dock with the bow a foot out of water and the wake piling up in huge, matching fans.

"Get down!" I screamed. One of the men aboard the yacht had leveled a rifle.

"They won't dare shoot — too much noise," hollered Bo. "They can't afford to attract attention!"

Bo's logic was very good. We didn't hear a report. The rifle had some kind of silencer.

The muzzle squirted flames, and the water to the right and left of us cast up tiny puffs of foam. The bullets were landing closer with each shot.

Orv swung the boat hard to port and cornered the island. The dock and the yacht disappeared behind the wall. I sat up and felt the wonder of a whole skin. We were in the clear.

I had my dime in my hand as Orv spun into the marina at Key Biscayne. Before he had touched a piling, I was ashore and sprinting for the red telephone booth to call Dad.

Halfway there two big men caught me. My legs continued to run the hundred in ten seconds flat, but I wasn't moving an inch. The men held me off the ground by the armpits.

"Ken Mullins?" they asked.

"Y-yes," I stammered.

They put me down and introduced themselves as Mr. O'Meara and Mr. Silvers. Mr. O'Meara handed me a slip of paper with a telephone number and told me to call Dad.

The light dawned. "You're from Mongoose?"

"We are," said Mr. Silvers. "We saw four boys steal aboard the Cobra yacht last night. We weren't certain it was you and your friends. When the crew arrived, we had to move away. We couldn't risk an encounter with Cobra then."

I remembered the two men Horseshoes had reported approaching the yacht. I went to the telephone booth, but I was no longer sprinting. My hips felt as if they were an arm's length apart, and my knees wobbled like a cat on a clothesline, I mean, I was scared blue.

I tried three times to get the dime into the coin slot above the telephone. I finally succeeded. But I fumbled it into the slot for quarters and had to start over.

I dialed, and Dad's voice came on after the first ring. When he heard who was calling, he didn't sound like

Dad. He sounded like a whole Father and Son dinner with everybody talking at once.

Dad wanted to know if Orv, Bo, Horseshoes, and I were all right. Then he asked what we were doing on Mystery Island, and he gave me the answer — wrecking his plans. I didn't get to say a word.

Dad said that Mongoose had been observing the island for more than a year. Last night he was ready to raid it, but Orv, Bo, Horseshoes, and I had fouled up everything. Dad wouldn't risk our lives. Now, he said, Cobra must be paid the ten million dollars. The money had arrived from Washington.

"It's too late!" I blurted. "Cobra wants a hundred million!"

There was a pause. "What do you mean?" demanded Dad.

"Everybody in Miami is going to get drugged hinking drilk!" I said.

"What?"

"I mean, drinking milk."

Then I told Dad about the lion and the memory pills and Mr. Schnitzer and the dairies being drugged. I described the island and the airplane and submarine they had ready for their getaway.

When I was done, Dad said: "I have five hundred men in the area. I can call upon the Coast Guard, the police, and the Air Force. We can stop most of the home milk deliveries. Now do exactly as I tell you, Ken. Have Bo, Orv, and Jerry telephone home and let their parents know they are unhurt. Then go to Orv's house and stay close to the pillbox. Don't go near the main roads — they'll be used for emergency cars only."

"Yes, sir," I said.

I reported my instructions to Bo, Orv, and Horseshoes. After they had spoken with their mothers, we piled in the Rod. We felt pretty good about V.A.C.U.U.M.'s first mission. We had saved Miami.

"If Ken's dad had raided Mystery Island," said Orv, "he might not have learned about the milk at all."

"Maybe the President will pin a medal on us," I said. "Boy, would Mom be proud!"

In the back seat, Bo was trying to cheer up Horseshoes.

"It was you or he," said Bo. "If you didn't shoot, we wouldn't have got away."

Nothing, however, helped. Horseshoes sat hunched up, looking small and full of pain.

Mrs. Davy was waiting outside the house when we arrived. She rushed to the car and threw her arms around Orv and asked a million questions. It was quite a while before any of us noticed Big Dog was gone.

"Mr. Vorhoose telephoned half an hour ago," Mrs. Davy explained. "He wanted to start for the car show right away. Honestly, I sometimes think antique car lovers are a trifle — well, loony!"

Orv was disappointed at the news. I knew his dad had promised to take him along the first time he entered Big Dog in a show.

"Where were they going — Orlando or Reservoir City?" asked Orv.

"Mr. Vorhoose hadn't made up his mind," said Mrs. Davy. "Dad said he'd telephone as soon as they arrived."

Orv dug his hands into his pockets gloomily. I slapped him on the back.

"So you missed a car show," I said. "But if you'd gone to Orlando or Reservoir City instead of to Mystery Island, you would have come back to — "

"Don't say it," said Orv.

"We could still overtake Big Dog," I suggested.

"Your dad told us to stay here," said Orv. "We stay."

I walked across the yard toward the pillbox. I had taken several steps before I realized Orv wasn't abreast of me.

"Orv — ?"

He was standing stock still. There was more in his expression than disappointment at missing Big Dog's first show.

He made a funny, confused motion with his arm, as if he wanted to push me away and call me to him.

"Ken," he said. "In the morning a rainbow is in the west."

I felt my scalp tingle, though as yet I didn't quite understand.

"A rainbow is in the western sky in the morning," explained Orv. "That guard said he saw one out the window. But the window faced east."

"What's the point?" asked Bo uneasily.

"The guard pretended to look at a rainbow that wasn't there," said Orv. "He turned his back on us and set aside his rifle."

My breath caught in my chest. I knew what was coming before Orv spoke again.

"They let us escape," he said.

A siren screamed in the distance. The police were hurrying to support Mongoose.

But where we stood, all was silence and dismay.

"The escape was too easy," said Orv.

"Why should Cobra allow us to get away?" objected Bo.

"To use us — and we fell into their hands at the perfect moment."

"Nonsense," said Bo. "To Cobra we were just a bunch of nervy kids."

"No," I said, for the explanation had thudded in my mind. "Mom's sleeping pills. Her name was on the bottles — Mrs. Carl Mullins. Mr. Schnitzer knew right away I was the son of Carl Mullins of Mongoose."

"Cobra has a book on every Mongoose agent in the Miami area," said Orv. "You can bet on that."

Above us a Coast Guard seaplane roared in the direction of Mystery Island.

"And I told Dad just what Mr. Schnitzer wanted me to — the memory drug was put into the milk," I said miserably. "All along Cobra has intended to spread the drug in another way."

"You can be sure Cobra has moved its headquarters off Mystery Island," said Bo. "Schnitzer and his gang are safe aboard the submarine or airplane right now."

Only Horseshoes found any comfort in our night of disaster.

"Then I didn't really kill the man in the tan suit?" he said.

"No," said Orv. "But if there's any doubt in your mind, the rifle will remove it."

He went to the Rod and took the rifle from the floor in back. Slowly he walked to the front of the car. He raised the rifle and aimed it over the hood.

He fired three rapid shots at the windshield.

The smoke cleared and we stared. The glass was unbroken.

"Blanks," said Orv. "The man in the tan suit ought to win an award for best actor of the year."

Five minutes ago we had been so puffed up with our

importance. V.A.C.U.U.M. had done what Mongoose couldn't do — discover how Cobra planned to carry out its threat against Miami!

Now we were just a bunch of kids who had done more harm than any four kids in history.

"They figured every step," I said. "They even had a boat handy for us to use so we didn't delay their time-table by swimming to the mainland."

"What'll we do?" said Horseshoes.

I knew what I must do. I went to the telephone. Nothing I'll ever attempt the rest of my life can compare with walking to that telephone. I had to tell Dad what a mess we'd made.

I dialed his office. I dialed home, and I dialed the number Mr. O'Meara had given me. No use. The operator cut in and said, "I'm sorry. That number is temporarily out of order." Dad had cut off all incoming calls.

I trudged back to Orv, Bo, and Horseshoes and told them.

"What'll we do?" I said.

13

"The Sleeper"

THE COMBINED FORCES of the police, the Coast Guard, the Air Force, and Mongoose were moving on Mystery Island and the milk trucks. It was too late to recall them.

And Cobra? Having staged the great bluff, Cobra was ready to execute its real plan somewhere else.

"V.A.C.U.U.M.!" said Bo in disgust. "Secret agents! What a laugh. We were errand boys for Cobra!"

Horseshoes and I muttered agreement. We wanted to sink into the grass.

Orv wasn't ready to give up, however.

"We've got to go back to the beginning," he said. "We have to start with the stranger in the blue car."

"That's what led us into all this trouble," objected Bo. "We chased him and he got away. Then we figured out that he had called Mystery Island. We should have stuck to inventing!"

"Maybe we read the clues wrong," said Orv stubbornly. "We missed something, or we failed to add things up correctly."

"What's to add up?" broke in Horseshoes. "The stranger wasn't twins. He was alone. Add him up and you get nothing we don't already know. Which is zip-zip-zero!"

Bo spoke, but I was no longer listening. Something stuck in the middle of my brain. The warm spot started and grew. Pretty soon some ideas were baking.

"You'll have to pardon me," I said. "I'm going into the pillbox and do some bak — er, thinking."

"If you get hungry, come into the kitchen," said Orv. "We'll be eating breakfast."

While Orv, Bo, and Horseshoes drowned their woes in milk and cereal, I sat down on the busted snow remover.

"Ken Mullins," I said to myself. "You want to be a secret agent. Well, there's no time like the present. So think!"

I thought harder than I'd ever thought before, even harder than during the physics final two weeks ago. When I got everything clear and straight in my head, I went into the kitchen.

"Mr. Vorhoose," I said, "is a sleeper."

"That's nice," said Bo. "No troubles with sleeping pills."

I ignored the remark.

"A sleeper," I explained, "is a person who is sent to live in a country by an enemy power. He becomes a citizen, makes friends, and lives normally. Perhaps he takes up a hobby, like collecting old coins or old cars. If his true country ever orders him, he performs some act — he blows up a bridge, steals secret documents, or assassinates the head of the government. Often his country never calls upon him, and he dies without anybody learning his true character.

"Are you saying Mr. Vorhoose is a Cobra sleeper?" asked Orv.

"I am," I answered. "We went wrong with our very first clue. The stranger used the telephone in the shop to make a local call all right. But it wasn't to Mystery Island. It was to a house ten blocks from here — Mr. Vorhoose's house."

Bo, Orv, and Horseshoes stopped shoveling in the cold cereal.

"The stranger," I said, "was carrying the memory powder. He had been instructed to stop here and call Mr. Vorhoose if he was in trouble."

Orv said, "After the stranger finished at the telephone,

he went into the paint barn with Big Dog. But he didn't do any damage."

"No," I said. "And that was where we went wrong with the second clue. We looked for something broken on Big Dog. Instead, we should have looked on the floor."

"The stranger dropped something?" asked Horseshoes.

"He emptied the memory powder into the new, dry cell battery. It was on the floor of the paint barn, remember?" I said. "Why do you suppose Mr. Vorhoose never let Mr. Davy hook up a new battery to any of his newly restored cars? Or even let Mr. Davy fill a new battery with sulphuric acid?"

"Why?" said Orv.

"It wasn't for the reason Mr. Vorhoose gives — that he likes to be the first one to start a newly restored car. That's pure hokum. This was all planned years ago — long before Mr. Vorhoose asked Orv's dad to restore an old car for him. He was building to the day when an empty battery had to be ready as an emergency hiding place for the memory drug!"

"It's all pretty far-fetched," said Bo.

"Mr. Vorhoose did get Dad out of the way by sending him to Jacksonville on the day the stranger stopped at the house," pointed out Orv. "And Mr. Schnitzer could have called Mr. Vorhoose last night and told him about us and that he planned to use us to throw Mongoose off the scent. That would account for Mr. Vorhoose making Dad start for the car show early, before we got back."

Orv was coming around to my side. So I pointed to a strange coincidence. Cobra's strike against Miami and the two old car shows fell on the same day. But Bo and Horseshoes still had to be convinced.

So I hit them with Cobra's real plan.

"One car show today is at Orlando," I said. "The other is at Reservoir City. If we start right now, we can still overtake Mr. Vorhoose and Orv's dad on the parkway. If Mr. Vorhoose has Mr. Davy take the Sunshine State Parkway to Orlando, well, he's innocent and I'm all wrong. But if Big Dog ends up at Reservoir City, we'll know."

"Just what is it we'll know?" asked Horseshoes impatiently.

"We'll know," I said, "that Mr. Vorhoose doesn't care about the car show. That part is only a cover. He'll be at Reservoir City for only one reason — *to dump the memory powder into Miami's water supply.*"

Nobody spoke for a few seconds. It was as if I'd knocked the wind out of them.

"My dad is in danger," said Orv softly.

"Not if we overtake them in time," I assured him. "The Rod can do it and — "

"The Rod stays here, and so do we," said Bo firmly.

"We've done enough harm already. I've had my fill of playing secret agent. Your reasoning is clever, Ken. But it isn't based on anything you can prove."

"Wait, Bo. I want to hear more," said Mrs. Davy. She had been listening by the sink. "Go on, Ken."

"Thanks, Mrs. Davy," I said. "I'll put it all together." I drew a deep breath and plunged into it.

"The stranger — I overheard my dad mention his name was Max Ripley — picked up the powder somewhere; let's say the railroad station or the airport. Ripley's instructions were to deliver the powder to Mr. Vorhoose's house. But he had to take a route laid out for him long ago — past Orv's house — in case Mongoose agents trailed him. Mongoose agents did trail him. Ripley spotted them and knew he couldn't make the delivery at Mr. Vorhoose's house. That would put the finger on the Cobra agent who was going to drug Miami's drinking water. So Ripley had to follow Cobra's emergency plan."

I paused briefly. When I had the rest of the details arranged in my mind, I went on.

"According to the emergency plan, Ripley was to make a telephone call from Mr. Davy's shop and hide the memory powder in Big Dog's empty battery. But he had to make his choice of Mr. Davy's shop appear like chance to the Mongoose agents trailing him. So he stopped first at a couple of houses down the block. He knew beforehand which families were away for the summer. And he knew Mr. Davy wouldn't be in his shop because Mr. Vorhoose had sent him up to Jacksonville to look over a Buick.

"When Ripley telephoned Mr. Vorhoose, he didn't have to say a word," I concluded. "Mr. Vorhoose knew Ripley was being followed and couldn't deliver the memory powder to his house. After hanging up, Ripley completed the emergency plan; he slipped the powder into the battery and fled."

"Then all along Mystery Island was nothing but a big beautiful decoy — a fake to mislead Mongoose!" said Bo.

"Exactly," I replied. "While Mongoose agents watched it night and day, the real center of the Cobra plot was Mr. Vorhoose's house!"

"If you're right," said Bo, "Mongoose still doesn't know that Mr. Vorhoose is a Cobra agent."

"We've got to overtake Mr. Vorhoose before he reaches Reservoir City," I said.

Bo, Orv, and Horseshoes broke from the breakfast table.

"Orville!" called Mrs. Davy.

Orv stopped short.

Mrs. Davy crossed the kitchen and gave him a quick kiss. "Be careful."

"Don't worry, Mom," said Orv. "We'll catch them. Dad will be okay."

We were V.A.C.U.U.M. again. We started for the Rod

as though nothing on this earth could stop us. We didn't get out the kitchen door.

"Sit down."

It was Max Ripley, the man who had started everything.

Nobody had a doubt about the gun in his hand.

It wasn't loaded with blanks, and he wasn't going to let us get away.

14

Mary Takes a Hand

"YOU HAVE BEEN MOST USEFUL, boys," said Max Ripley. "Cobra is grateful. Now, alas, there is no more you can do. So make yourselves comfortable for a few hours."

He spoke with mock politeness. He had no need for threatening tones or words. He had the gun.

He gave the gun a businesslike flick toward the empty chair at the breakfast table.

"Mrs. Davy, please sit down," he said. "I apologize for causing you any fright."

"Don't bother," said Mrs. Davy.

Mrs. Davy is a small, quiet woman. I'd never heard her raise her voice in anger before. Her fingers moved to the rolling pin by the sink.

Bo snarled one of his best snarls, and Ripley pointed the gun at him in alarm. In that second, Mrs. Davy slipped the rolling pin under her apron.

"Mrs. Davy," I said under my breath. "Sit down and kindly don't get ideas."

Mrs. Davy sat down. She held the rolling pin in her lap and pretended she was about to pass out with fright.

Ripley grinned. His lips curled back and his teeth flashed as if somebody had raised the lid of a grand piano.

"It won't be long," he promised. "Three hours, perhaps four, and the memory powder will be flowing through the pipes of Miami."

In the hall behind him a shadow moved. I thought it might be one of the twins. But the head which finally edged into view wasn't brunette. It was blonde, and it belonged to Mary Evans.

I tried to signal that Ripley had a gun. My cheeks twitched an S.O.S.

"What's with you?" demanded Ripley.

"Something is in my eye," I said.

I poked a forefinger into my eye and wiggled my thumb like a trigger.

"Say — "

Ripley spun even as Mary was striking. The edge of her hand slammed his wrist upward. The gun went off.

V.A.C.U.U.M. surged from the table. Mrs. Davy aimed

the rolling pin at Ripley. Bo got in the way and it smacked him on the base of the skull. He went down faster than he'd risen.

The gun exploded again. Horseshoes, who was up like a spring popping, yelped and dropped to the floor, holding his knee. Orv snagged a foot in Horseshoes' armpit and sailed headlong into the pantry, starting a landslide of soup cans.

By the time I'd picked my way over the bodies, Mary and Ripley were battling furiously in the hall. The gun skidded into the living room. Ripley lunged after it.

"Hold him, Mary!" I shouted. "I'm coming!"

I charged for Ripley. He met me halfway, flying through the air upside down. His elbow struck my chin. We crumpled in a heap just inside the living room.

He struggled free and hurled himself wildly at Mary. He cast aside the arts of hand-to-hand combat and relied upon brute strength for a quick victory. I guess he didn't believe a teen-age girl could throw him.

Mary shouted, "*Sa!*"

I watched dizzily. The room seemed to be going around and around. It wasn't, really. Only Ripley was.

The Cobra agent was soaring and circling and looping. Mary was shouting Japanese fighting words and stamping her feet like a Spanish dancer.

Ripley survived a dozen crash landings before Mary threw him for good.

"Whew! Lucky for me he lost his head," she said, panting. "What's happening? I came over to hear about Mystery Island and saw this man listening outside the kitchen window."

"He tried to stop us," I said. "I'll bring you up to date another time."

In the kitchen Orv was dusting off soup cans. Bo was on his feet rubbing his skull groggily. Mrs. Davy knelt beside Horseshoes, who lay on the kitchen floor. "My knee," he groaned. "My knee."

"Is he wounded?" I asked.

"He's slightly crippled," said Orv. "He banged his knee on the leg of the table trying to help Mary."

"I'm glad he didn't mix in," I said. "He might really have got hurt."

Horseshoes couldn't walk. Bo nursed a lump on his head the size of a dime-store turtle. Orv and I had to stop Mr. Vorhoose alone.

Having directed Mary to guard Ripley till Bo recovered, Orv and I sprinted for the Rod. In my excitement I forgot about Davy-power and turned the key to the right. The Rod's back end dropped to the ground with a whoosshh!

The rear wheels were still bounding over the yard as Orv and I jumped out. We chased through his dad's crop of antique cars.

"What runs?" I yelled.

"This one," replied Orv, hopping behind the tiller of a 1911 Maxwell fire chief's car.

I whirled the crank. The motor kicked over and growled like a regular little tiger.

"We'll never make it to Reservoir City in this," I bellowed above the banging of the two-cylinder engine.

"Nope!" sang Orv. "We're going to the airstrip. "We'll fly the De Havilland to Reservoir City. Your dad said to stay off the main roads."

"Yeah," I hollered as we chugged off. "But take *some* road."

"Short cut!" cried Orv, and hunched forward.

The Dade City airstrip is four miles from Orv's house — for normal drivers. By making his own way across the lawns and zig-zagging through pine forests, Orv trimmed off a mile.

I hung on with both hands and winced. Within sight of the airstrip, the little engine clinked, clanked, and clunked.

"Out of gas!" wailed Orv.

We covered the last half mile to the De Havilland on foot. My tongue was dragging as I spun the propeller and fell headfirst into the cockpit.

I'd barely got straightened out and strapped in when Orv had us airborne. We swung around and followed Route 1 north to the Palmetto Expressway. A stream of Army trucks was moving south. To the east, Mystery Island was a wee blob of green and brown ringed by Coast Guard vessels.

At the Sunset Drive exit to the Palmetto Expressway Orv banked and slowed. Ahead lay Reservoir City, Cobra's target.

Reservoir City is a city in name only. Actually it is a mammoth water treatment plant enclosed by a high wire fence. Water is pumped from the Everglades and then softened, filtered, and stored temporarily in two huge tanks, or reservoirs. The tanks hold ten million gallons each, or enough to supply Miami for eight hours.

In junior high school I'd written a science paper on Reservoir City. I knew the only point at which Mr. Vorhoose could introduce the memory drug into the drinking water was at the storage tanks. The tanks were buried two-thirds underground. But each had several air pipes, or vents, projecting upward four feet. From the sky the vents looked like giant white mushrooms. We had to stop Mr. Vorhoose before he poured the powder down them!

I checked my watch. It was almost eight o'clock, two hours before the antique cars had to be in place for the judging on the front lawn. For the past seven years, the Miami Vintage Car Association had held its spring meets at Reservoir City. On meet days the guards admitted anyone with an antique car.

Orv passed over the length of the plant, circled, and dipped a wing as a signal to me.

On the lawn in front of the administration building were Mr. Davy's white pickup truck and trailer.

Orv pounded the plywood side of the plane, which meant he was going to land. The wide span of lawn that seemed majestically large from the ground suddenly shrank to a door mat.

"Orv can do it," I thought, gulping. "He's a genius."

We flew south for three blocks and circled. Getting the wind right was tricky, and Orv had to make his approach at a dangerous angle. If he didn't land us perfectly, we'd end up as water softener.

The De Havilland slanted down. Our speed slowed to about forty miles an hour swooping past a supermarket. Shoppers screamed up at us as if they didn't want to be saved.

Passing the maintenance shop in Reservoir City, we brushed a cypress tree. The whole plane trembled and went into a nose dive. Orv jerked her up frantically. We hit the ground on one wheel, snapped it off, and spun to a stop.

"Orv!" I said. "Great going!"

And it was, even if we'd left one wing wrapped around a royal palm. The broken wheel and a lot of other parts I couldn't immediately identify were scattered behind us for a hundred yards.

We jumped to the ground and ran. If we didn't move fast, some of the water plant workers would be on our necks for tearing up the grass.

Big Dog had been rolled out of the white trailer. Mr. Vorhoose was holding the battery. He looked as if he were going to drop it on Mr. Davy's head.

"Dad, watch out!" shouted Orv.

Mr. Davy was stooped over in order to remove the panel above the running board which hid the battery compartment.

"The battery!" said Orv. "It's filled with a drug that will make people believe today is yesterday!"

Mr. Davy is a very calm man. He never becomes upset. "Son," he said, "are you all right? That was a mighty peculiar method of getting to a car show."

"Dad, listen to me!" Orv pleaded. "That battery is filled with a terrible drug!"

Mr. Vorhoose smiled at us as if we were little boys whose game of cops and robbers had begun to irk the grownups.

"If you don't believe us, unscrew the battery caps," I said.

Mr. Vorhoose placed the battery on the ground. He unscrewed the caps.

"Would you care to make an inspection?" he taunted.

We looked into each cell. *They were all empty.*

"That battery was filled with memory powder while it

was on the floor of the paint barn five days ago," said Orv. "It must have secret chambers. Break it apart, Dad!"

"The battery I kept in the paint barn was for Mr. Craig's Lincoln roadster," said Mr. Davy. "I installed it yesterday morning. This battery I purchased myself last night."

Orv and I watched each other's face grow red.

There was no question that we had been wrong about the battery. Cobra was again a step ahead of V.A.C.U.U.M. We couldn't seem to catch up. It was like a nightmare.

"Now I want you to apologize to Mr. Vorhoose," said Mr. Davy sternly. "And then pick up the mess you made on the lawn."

15

Two Against Cobra

Because Mr. Davy insisted, Orv and I apologized to Mr. Vorhoose.

"Sorry," said Orv.

"Sorry," I said.

One word was all we could get out between clenched teeth.

Mr. Vorhoose smiled. He shook hands forgivingly. But his eyes above the smile were hard chips of hate.

Orv and I walked toward the wreckage of the De Havilland. Mr. Vorhoose's eyes had given him away. Yet we were powerless to do anything.

"The memory powder is hidden on Big Dog," said

Orv. "It isn't in the battery, but it's somewhere. As proof, we have Max Ripley's attempt to stop us from coming here."

"Your dad checked the car over. He found nothing, remember?" I said, thoroughly confused.

"Yes, but Dad didn't start the engine," said Orv. "And it still hasn't been started."

We slowed until we had come to a halt. We had to act as if we were busy while keeping our backs to Big Dog. We listened for the engine to start.

So we counted the airplane parts that lay strewn over the grass.

"How many pieces do you make?" asked Orv.

"Three hundred and twelve," I said, "counting the wing on the palm tree as one."

"That means I landed with less than half an airplane," said Orv proudly.

"What's delaying your dad?" I said anxiously. "He ought to have the battery hooked up by now!"

Across the lawn a crowd of workers from the water plant had collected around the carcass of the De Havilland. Among them was a large man with a ten-gallon stomach pulled over his belt. He was gesturing and moving about importantly, getting to the bottom of things.

"We're in for it," I said.

We couldn't let the heavy man lock us away before Mr. Vorhoose tried to start Big Dog.

"Don't run or turn," warned Orv. "Make believe we're going toward him. Act friendly and walk backward!"

We were midway between the De Havilland and Big Dog, about fifty yards from each. The heavy man bellowed and beckoned. We nodded, waved cheerfully, and walked backward. For ten yards we fooled him. Then he caught on. He came at us like a wounded hippo, but we had gained a few precious seconds.

"This meet is for antique cars, not for old plane parts," he said, puffing angrily.

He said he was Mr. Bragg, the caretaker, and he expressed some very strong opinions. I gathered he didn't approve of airplanes digging up his lawn and knocking over his water sprinklers.

We apologized for all we were worth and promised never to do it again. Mr. Bragg demanded to see Orv's pilot's license.

As Orv reached into his pocket, an engine started. It sounded like the Rod. A four-cylinder engine makes a special kind of chuffing noise.

I had to peek over my shoulder to make certain it was really Big Dog. Mr. Vorhoose sat in the driver's seat. Mr. Davy, wrench in hand, looked puzzled.

Big Dog's engine has eight cylinders, which are set in two parallel rows of four. The cylinders slant inward to the crankshaft at the bottom, forming a V; thus the name V-8 engine. A V-8 runs smoothly. Big Dog's V-8

sounded like the Rod's four cylinders chuffing away.

"You have an hour to scrape up that wreck," said Mr. Bragg. He hitched up his belly and stomped off.

An eight-cylinder engine that sounded like a four-cylinder engine . . .

"Orv," I said, "I've got it!"

"You said that about the battery," Orv reminded me.

"Name the parts of a car's electrical system," I said.

Orv rattled them off. "Switch, battery, points, coil — "

"Enough!" I said, holding up a hand. "Now, what does a snake do?"

"It bites," offered Orv.

"It *coils!*" I said. "The stranger, Max Ripley. Well, he carried a coil which was an exact copy of the real thing, on the outside. Inside, it was filled with memory powder. He was delivering it to Mr. Vorhoose when he saw the Mongoose agents trailing him. So he stopped at your house, the emergency hiding place. He had to work fast to exchange the fake coil for the real one, and he did. Because Mr. Vorhoose never allowed your dad to test his cars, Cobra knew the fake coil would not be discovered till Big Dog was on the grounds of Reservoir City!"

Behind us Big Dog's engine had died.

"Don't look yet. Let me finish," I said. "I heard Mr. Vorhoose running the engine while you were talking to Mr. Bragg. Big Dog has two coils. Each coil boosts the voltage for one row of four cylinders, right? Now, if one coil was a fake, what would the motor sound like?"

"Well one row of cylinders wouldn't fire," said Orv. "So Big Dog would sound like the Rod, because only four cylinders would be working."

"And that's exactly what Big Dog sounded like!" I said.

"I heard a four-cylinder engine chuffing away," said Orv. "What are we waiting for?"

We spun around, ready to tackle Mr. Vorhoose high and low. But Mr. Davy was alone by Big Dog.

"Where's Mr. Vorhoose?" Orv said, running up.

"One of the coils didn't work," answered Mr. Davy. "Mr. Vorhoose thought some rust on a terminal was causing the trouble. He went to the maintenance shop for a piece of sandpaper."

I peered under Big Dog's dashboard where the two coils are fastened. A coil looks like a small can of shaving foam painted black. One was missing.

"He took the bad coil with him," said Mr. Davy.

"Dad!" yelled Orv. "That coil is a dummy! It's filled with the memory drug!"

The last words trailed off as Orv and I raced across the grass toward the maintenance shop.

The shop was crammed with everything but people.

"Mr. Vorhoose never came here," I said to Orv. "When

he got out of sight behind those water-softener units, he must have doubled back to the buildings."

"He's on his way to the storage tanks," said Orv. "Look!"

Mr. Vorhoose appeared fleetingly at the top of the stairs alongside the administration building. Then he disappeared inside, moving toward the covered third-floor ramp where the filter control tables stood. The ramp connected with the grass-covered tops of the storage tanks.

My speed across the lawn to the stairs would have won the state 100-yard-dash finals. I was racing for a lot more than school glory, and my legs knew it. They carried me up the stairs four at a bound.

The stairway was deserted. The offices and most of the work areas were deserted too. All the men who could steal away from their jobs for a few minutes had done so. They were on the lawn, gaping at the De Havilland.

"What a twist!" I thought. "V.A.C.U.U.M. helps Cobra again! Mr. Vorhoose couldn't have arranged a better way to draw off attention."

With no one on the third floor to challenge him, he had a clear path to the storage tanks!

As I gained the top of the stairs, Orv was a flight below. I saw Mr. Vorhoose at the far end of the ramp. He was walking calmly. He might have been a harmless sightseer unintentionally wandering into the forbidden area.

He was thirty yards ahead of me as he stepped onto the grass above the tanks. He looked skyward.

A whirring sound grew louder and louder. Through the open sides of the ramp I saw a helicopter approach. It was painted the same copper color as the uniforms of the guards on Mystery Island.

Cobra had planned every detail. Mr. Vorhoose was to escape by air!

I hurled myself over the remaining yards in a flying tackle. A sixth sense warned Mr. Vorhoose. He twisted around, his eyes wide with surprise but not fear. Side-stepping, he dealt me a chopping blow behind the ear.

I landed on the grass, my head ringing like a field of cowbells. Above me, a rope ladder dropped from the helicopter and danced in the air.

"Mongoose has the place surrounded!" I bawled.

Mr. Vorhoose sneered at the lie. I dived for him again and hit him with my shoulder before he could unscrew the top off the coil. He rode with the thrust skilfully. As I floundered past, he kicked me in the ribs.

I wobbled upright, hardly able to breathe. My side ached from the kick and my head didn't feel much better. The roar of the helicopter pounded in my ears. I was in very good shape for a stretcher or reinforcements.

Orv dashed out from the covered ramp and just as quickly dashed back. Dirt sprayed at his heels. Somebody in the helicopter was shooting!

"Keep close to Mr. Vorhoose," I told myself. "Cobra won't risk hitting their own man."

"Get him, Ken!" hollered Orv. "It's all up to you!"

I wished it were all up to somebody else. Mr. Vorhoose was knocking me silly with one hand.

"*Sa!*" I shouted in desperation. I didn't know what I said, but Mary knew, and so did Mr. Vorhoose. He thought he was being attacked by a full-fledged judo expert. He froze.

I locked my legs around him and hooked an arm under his chin in a choke hold. We tumbled on the grass with me underneath.

The rope ladder dipped toward us, and Mr. Vorhoose grabbed it with his free hand. I had delayed him long enough to upset Cobra's timetable. The pilot of the helicopter had panicked. He was ready to leave, with or without Mr. Vorhoose.

I was lifted off the ground. Mr. Vorhoose had to bear both of us with one hand. His other hand held the unopened coil.

"He can't do it," I thought, as we rose into the air. "He's got to let go of the ladder, or drop the coil and hang on with both hands."

Mr. Vorhoose did neither.

He wrenched his body to one side. The coil came at me like a pile driver.

I saw a starry burst of light . . . and then darkness.

16

"Just Fine"

I OPENED MY EYES and everything went white.

"You're in Memorial Hospital," said Dad. "How do you feel?"

"As if I'm lying down," I answered weakly.

Dad stood at the foot of my bed. Mom sat on a chair near my pillow. Hurriedly she slipped a moist ball of handkerchief into her handbag and smiled at me.

"I'll leave you alone," said a nurse. Her white uniform blended with the white walls. She closed the door softly, and I scarcely knew she was gone.

"What happened, Dad?"

"You got hit with this," he said, holding up the coil. He pointed to the dent in one side.

I touched my head. It was wrapped in bandages.

"Mr. Vorhoose dropped the coil when he hit you. Orv grabbed it. The powder is safe in Mongoose headquarters, along with Mr. Schnitzer and a dozen of Cobra's lesser lights."

"I'm sorry about Mystery Island," I mumbled. "It was a wild goose chase."

Dad laughed. "Cobra fooled Mongoose for months with the island," he said. "We watched it while the Cobra operation against Miami was being run from the Vorhoose house. There was nothing on the island but a lot of fake trees and a big control room."

"Wasn't there a submarine for Mr. Schnitzer's getaway?"

"No, nor an airplane," said Dad. "They were simply pictures that Schnitzer threw on the television screen to mislead you. He knew you'd report everything you learned to me."

"I don't understand that part," I said. "He had the pictures of the submarine and airplane ready to telecast, as if he expected us."

"He expected someone," said Dad. "Cobra's plan was to kidnap a Mongoose agent. Schnitzer was to show him the pictures and make him believe the island was the center of the entire plot. Naturally, the kidnaped agent would be told that the milk, not the water, would be drugged, and then allowed to escape. So while Mongoose threw all its manpower against the island and the dairies, Reservoir City would be left unguarded."

"When V.A.C.U.U.M. fell into his lap," I said, "Mr. Schnitzer decided to use us instead of kidnaping a Mongoose agent!"

"That's the way it happened," said Dad. "Schnitzer was very indignant when we captured him. He insisted he had done nothing wrong, and in fact he hadn't — yet. But he talked his head off when we told him we had Vorhoose — "

"You caught Mr. Vorhoose!" I exclaimed.

"Yes, thanks to Mr. Davy."

"Who?" I said in disbelief.

"Five days ago," said Dad, "I gave Fred Davy a telephone number where I could be reached in any emergency."

"But at Reservoir City, Mr. Davy acted as though Orv and I were nuts accusing Mr. Vorhoose," I said.

"He thought you were," said Dad, "till he saw the Cobra helicopter above the water tanks. He called me, and I ordered three Marine jet helicopters up from Key West. They forced Vorhoose down near Sarasota."

"Carl," said Mom, rising. "Let Ken rest." She clasped my hand tightly. "We'll see you in the morning."

Dad waved good-bye from the door.

"Did V.A.C.U.U.M. do all right?" I called.

"You boys were just fine," said Dad.

"*Fine!*" Mom scolded. She turned to me and said, "Your father is bursting he's so proud."

"Go easy, dear," said Dad. "He'll want a medal and his picture in the newspapers. Then there won't be anything secret about his being a secret agent."

I blew Mom a kiss as she went out. I guess a boy never understands his mother. Last year she screamed all over the house when I wanted a motorcycle. "Too dangerous," she said. Yet when I fall from a helicopter, all she does is cry a little and smile a lot.

The nurse let in V.A.C.U.U.M. "You boys have ten minutes," she said. "Don't get the patient excited."

"Don't worry," said Orv. "We've had our excitement this week."

Orv, Bo, and Horseshoes crowded close to the bed, beaming over their neckties.

"Mary sends regards," said Orv. "She's at a judo tourney in North Miami. She'll be by later."

"I hope she brings a blue ribbon with her," I said.

Mary at a judo tourney . . . Everything seemed normal again, as if V.A.C.U.U.M. had never come up against Cobra.

"You fell eight feet after Mr. Vorhoose socked you with the fake coil," said Orv. "You should have had a little pocket parachute."

"Stick it in the spy-catching machine," I said drowsily. "We never did invent one."

"We've been thinking on the subject," said Orv. "It won't only be for catching spies. It will have equipment for battling every kind of criminal."

"If we housed it in a sixteen-ton armored truck, we'd have room for a lot of stuff," said Horseshoes.

"Sounds good," I said, yawning. I closed my eyes.

"With a super engine, say eight hundred horsepower, we could race right to the scene of the crime," said Orv.

"A rolling police station," I breathed.

"It'd have all kinds of cameras," said Bo.

"And a two-way radio," said Orv, "and everything needed to take fingerprints and make blood tests . . . and . . ." His voice faded.

My eyelids grew heavier and heavier. Words rose and fell around me.

"Underwater diving gear . . ."

"And tear gas . . ."

". . . X-ray . . ."

"Summer vacation has only begun," I thought sleepily. "Plenty of time to build a spy-catching machine . . . Orv's . . . a genius . . ."